COLD BLOOD

What Reviewers Say About
Genevieve McCluer's Work

Olivia

"There's a playfulness at times, but then the seriousness of the situation hits the reader square in the face. At the halfway mark it suddenly took off for me. There was one heck of a surprise, that I did not see coming at all. I enjoyed the story and would like to read more in this world."—*Kitty Kat's Book Blog*

Thor: Daughter of Asgard

"Norse mythology intrudes on a bubbly romance in this light adventure from McCluer. ...Readers will come for the gender bending mythology and stay for the light romance."—*Publishers Weekly*

My Date with a Wendigo

"*My Date with a Wendigo* is a sweet, second chance romance at its furry little heart."—*Wicked Cool Flight*

A Fae Tale

"This is an unusual tale, but a very enjoyable one. It's funny and a bit kooky, but very sweet and romantic too. Genevieve McCluer writes great humorous prose and I found myself giggling out loud a few times in the course of reading this book. Her characters are well defined and fun, and she makes her secondary characters come to life as much as the main protagonists. An enjoyable read."
—*Kitty Kat's Book Blog*

By the Author

A Fae Tale

Thor: Daughter of Asgard

Olivia

My Date with a Wendigo

Cold Blood

COLD BLOOD

by

Genevieve McCluer

2022

COLD BLOOD

© 2022 By Genevieve McCluer. All Rights Reserved.

ISBN 13: 978-1-63679-195-1

This Trade Paperback Original Is Published By
Bold Strokes Books, Inc.
P.O. Box 249
Valley Falls, NY 12185

First Edition: April 2022

CREDITS
EDITOR: BARBARA ANN WRIGHT
PRODUCTION DESIGN: SUSAN RAMUNDO
COVER DESIGN BY TAMMY SEIDICK

Acknowledgments

Thank you to Jessica, Danny, Alexandra, and Kasian for all of your support and help, and to my editor, Barbara.

CHAPTER ONE

I stride into the bar, looking around. It's seedy, dank, dark, and smells of BO, piss, and stale peanuts. It's exactly the sort of place a vampire would hunt for prey. The sort of bar where people could disappear, and the next day, everyone would forget who they'd ever been. It's one of my favorite places to hunt.

In any other city.

This is the fifth bar I've checked out, and everyone inside seems to be an old drunk. I spent a good part of the last year clearing out Toledo, and when someone went to any seedy bar there, they had—at least before I was there too long—a good chance of catching the eye of a leech. They were everywhere, then, feeding on the desperate junkies who made up half the city. Maybe that was why they'd gotten so careless.

But I've been in Toronto for three days, and I haven't found so much as a whiff of a vampire. I know they're here, I have a good lead, even if it's old enough to have gone cold, and there are other hunters in town. I've kept my distance, but I'm starting to run out of other options. Someone has to know something, and I need answers. He came here fourteen years ago. It's taken me this long to track him down. I'm not losing him.

I walk over to the bar, taking my hat off as I sit.

The bartender takes his sweet time coming over to me, so I take another look around the place. It's even uglier than before. To my right, there's a fat man in a tank top barely able to keep himself in his chair. Behind me, there are a few older men laughing and drinking. At a table to my left is a couple actually eating in this dive. No accounting for taste.

The slob at the bar turns, seeming to notice me. He waves, his movements so sloppy that he bumps into a bowl of nuts and knocks over a cup of toothpicks. I pick up the eleven, individually wrapped toothpicks, put them back in the container, and right it. "I think you've had too much to drink," I say.

"Must've," he slurs. "Maybe you should take me home."

It is better than I tended to get in Toledo, but I don't feel it'll help my search. "How about we call you a cab?"

"Oh, don't mind Otto," the bartender says. He's an older man with grey hair and glasses. It's possible he's been here long enough to have some answers.

"I don't want to see someone drink himself to death."

He looks drunk Otto up and down. "Let me call you a cab." He turns back to me. "And what about you? Can I get you anything, or did you come here to scare my customers off?"

I've had to grow used to it to avoid suspicion, but I've never developed a taste for alcohol. "Sure, a Coors."

He grabs a bottle from under the bar, pops off the lid with his bare hand, and hands it to me. Neat trick. I could do it too, but his hands look calloused from years of practicing. "That's quite an accent you've got."

"I suppose so." I sip the beer, trying not to let the discomfort show on my face. It's weak enough that the taste isn't quite revolting, but I cannot understand how people ever grow an appetite for the stuff.

"Where you from?"

"Toledo," I say.

"That in Afghanistan?"

I sigh but force a smile. "It's in Ohio."

He nods, his eyes narrowing, taking me in. I'm wearing jeans and a long-sleeve shirt with a leather jacket, so there's not much to see, but that never seems to stop old guys from judging me. He apparently decides better than to ask whatever wretched thing crawled into his head to make him ask all that in the first place. I was used to far worse back in the States. "What brings you to our fair city?"

Finally, an excuse to get information. "I'm looking for this man." I take the crumpled photo from my pocket and slide it onto the bar. In it, a platoon of American soldiers sit together in mostly full uniforms. One's missing a shirt and another has his unbuttoned. They're posed with their weapons at the ready, grinning like lunatics at the camera. I tap the one with the open shirt.

He stares at the picture, his eyes narrowing. "Who is he?"

I can't tell if there's any recognition. He has a good poker face. Another skill I had to learn to get by in America. "He owes child support." Barring a few assholes, which I have no way of knowing if this guy is one, it's a story that works with most people. No one likes the idea of a kid being left to starve because his father is too much of a coward.

"You the mom?"

"It make a difference?"

He grunts. "I can't say I recognize him."

Is he lying? I stare at him, studying his eyes. They're brown, and if I didn't know better, I'd say they looked honest. He has laugh lines all around them. I nod. "All right."

"You're sure he's in town?"

"He was. I haven't heard anything in a long time." If I am honest about the date, it will raise some questions on the child support, so I keep it vague.

He purses his lips, studying me before finally nodding. "It's a big city."

"So I'm learning." It has been three days, and I haven't learned a thing. I bought a new machete and some flex cuffs but barely have enough money left for a few more drinks. "Know any good poker games in town?" I ask with a light chuckle. I can't exactly get an ordinary job, and it's looking like I'll have to bribe a lot of people to get the slightest bit of information. Three days, so many questions, and not a single vampire. It doesn't make sense. What makes Toronto so special?

"I usually go down to Windsor. They have a nice casino there."

It is doable in a pinch. I should've stopped on the way when I saw the casino, but I wanted to hurry. I'd been so sure I finally had him. Years of killing vampires and hunting for this bastard, and I finally have a clue where he is, only for it to all be fruitless. "I'll keep it in mind."

"Hell, maybe your ex is there. It's where I'd go if I wanted to avoid everyone and had to make sure I didn't have money."

I want to throw up at the idea of him being my ex. Or maybe it's the beer. "Thank you."

"Anything else I can get you?"

I gaze meaningfully at my drink as if I strongly want another but am trying to resist. "No. I have work to do. Thank you, though." I stand, pay my tab, grab my hat, and walk back outside.

No one even follows me.

What does it take in this town to find a vampire? Sighing, I put the hat on and stare at the starry sky. It's a perfect night for a hunt. They should be out in numbers.

I can practically smell the blood in the air.

But there's nothing.

It doesn't make any sense. I kick the gravel of the parking lot, knocking up dust. I've been in dozens of towns, and none of them have been this empty. Three days is plenty of time to at least catch a hint of something supernatural.

Could it be because that monster was here? He didn't seem like he had any sort of control when I met him. It couldn't be possible that he's managed to corral a mass of leeches into any semblance of order. But what else can make Toronto so unusual?

I'll just have to find that out, won't I? Since no one seems to want to attack me, I climb into my beat-up old Chevy pickup and hit the road. There are plenty of places to still look, and with how weird Toronto is, it might not be dangerous to do so.

That makes it boring, but it could make finding things out easier.

I drive to the nearest blood bank. It's always a gamble, but maybe it will explain why all the hunting grounds are empty. I suppose I'll have to hope that it's not as useless as they tend to be.

CHAPTER TWO

The first blood bank I find on Google Maps is in the basement of a hospital. The place stinks of embalming fluid and cleaning supplies. There's no way any vampires would come in here, right? As sensitive as their senses are, it would be overwhelming. The fluorescent lights are so bright I can barely stand it.

I have to take a few turns and consult a number of signs, but I finally manage to find a door to the right room. Inside, I find an equally sterile and painfully bright room. There doesn't seem to be anyone in it, but there's a desk out front and a bell on it. I ring it and promptly have to ring it again to make sure.

Twice should be plenty. I know I rang it.

I stare at the bell.

I hit it one more time and groan. That was completely unnecessary. Now they're going to think I'm impatient or playing around, and neither one is useful.

A woman wearing hospital scrubs and a lab coat pops in through a door in the back. "Can I help you?" she asks, eyeing me as if I'm someone who kept repeatedly ringing their bell when they were trying to get work done.

I try a smile but quickly give up, hiding my teeth. I've never had a great smile, and I swear it's only grown less sincere-looking. I have had years practicing this conversation, almost a decade at this point, and it never gets any less awkward. How do you ask someone if they're breaking the law to provide food to monsters? You either sound crazy or like a cop. Often both. "Has anyone else been coming around here lately?" I try. "Like, who doesn't work for the hospital?"

She chuckles and eyes me, seeming to study every inch. It makes me feel rather exposed. "What kind of question is that?"

It's better than telling me to fuck off, which is about what I got half the time in these places. I'll have to play this cautiously. She's already suspicious, and I feel like, if I ask anything too strange or probe too hard, she might not give me anything at all, but on the other hand, if I make it too vague, then I may miss out on details that can get me a lot further. Bars are so much easier. At least in every other city. There are enough of them that losing access to one isn't nearly as big of a hurdle, and they don't tend to freak out half as quickly when questioned.

Which leaves me one option. Generally, the best one, but I hate doing it. It feels vulgar. "Well, if I'm not the only one coming, it means I'm not barking up the wrong tree."

She stares harder. Am I taking the wrong tack? It's always tough to predict.

I should've tried the picture. Pretending he's the father of my child always hurts, but it's the easiest way to get answers. "I can take my money elsewhere." I've already picked my method of attack, and it's too late to try to change it, so all I can do is double down.

"You do know what city you're in, right?"

Now it's my turn to stare. However, I'm not sizing her up, I'm simply at a complete loss. What could that possibly mean? "I'm sorry?"

"I suppose you're not from around here. Your kind doesn't shop at the blood banks here. There are places that cater specifically to you."

"I'm not..." I take a deep breath, stopping myself. She has to think I'm shopping for blood, even if it means I have to endure the indignity of her believing I'm a leech. "I'm not sure what you mean."

She chuckles. "All I know is, once I started here, I was handed a flyer and told to give it to anyone who looked all sickly and wanted to buy blood."

"I look sickly?"

She shrugs. "A little. Maybe not as pale as most. The accent is pretty vampiric, though."

It takes every fiber of my being not to lash out. My accent is vampiric? What does that mean? I'm not Romanian. Is any foreigner automatically a vampire? "What's this flyer?" I ask, trying to keep the anger out of my voice. Sickly and vampiric? I shudder.

"Gimme a minute," she says and goes back through the door.

I look around. There's not a proper waiting room, only two chairs and a table. Other than that, there's the counter and a number of cabinets behind it. Nothing much to investigate, and it's not like they'd have any files relevant to old vampires anyway.

Before I can sit, she comes back out holding a piece of printer paper. "This should be it. Here you go."

I take it from her, staring at it. All it says is, Blood Delivery, and a phone number. I turn back to her, trying not to let my confusion show too much. What is this? Is this why there aren't so many vampires hunting in town? "This is legit?"

"We're not allowed to sell anymore. I get a bit for referring you, though, so that'll be nice."

I gulp. Right, she thinks I'm ordering from them. Well, I suppose I am. How else am I going to see their clientele? He must be one of them. "Are there any other services like this?"

She shrugs. "I think there are a couple. That was the first flyer I found in the back."

I shake my head, struggling to form words. I open my mouth to question her but close it again and narrow my eyes. What the hell is going on in this city?

She shrugs again. "It's none of my business. Back in Quebec, I got a bunch of you lot, and now I don't have to deal with that, and I get paid without having to break any rules. I'm not gonna complain."

None of this is making any sense. "I just call this number?"

"Like ordering a pizza. Or do they not have that where you're from?"

I grunt in acknowledgment and head out the door, unable to take my eyes off the paper. I've never heard of anything like this. There are nests of vampires all over the world. For a species that's supposed to be endangered, it's disturbing how common they are, but I suppose it doesn't take much for them to reproduce. I touch my throat, far too easily able to imagine it. One night and there's a new monster. Don't have to wait nine months and a lifetime raising them.

I've been trying to keep up with their growth and keep the population down, but they must be reproducing faster than I'm killing them if there's enough for this kind of organization.

In so many cities, there've been groups of them living together and hunting together. I've seen all kinds of societies of these monsters but nothing corporate. It feels wrong. There's something about Toronto that's different from anyplace else I've been, and I don't trust it. It makes my blood run cold.

All I have to do is call. I head back to the parking lot and grab my phone from my pocket. I press in the first number and hear footsteps behind me.

I'm in a parking lot of a hospital, so it's not that unusual, but something about it puts me on edge. More steps move with them, not quite in time but moving in formation. At least some training, then; no one naturally moves like that. They're trying to keep quiet, but their training isn't quite good enough. Probably not professionals.

I spin, dropping my phone and the flyer as one leaps at me. I manage to catch his hand, stopping the cleaver a mere foot from my throat. Not a practical weapon, but he looks like he knows what he's doing. He's snarling, his face twisted into a mask of anger. I've never seen him before in my life, so I'm not sure what I did to deserve the resentment. He's pale but not vampire pale, and his hair is close-cropped and brown, with more on his upper lip than the top of his head.

I shove him away, but another one moves for me. He has a machete, and another one has an axe, moving with him in a pincer, trying to take me from either side. I rush the one with the machete, slugging him in the stomach.

He drops the machete, and I grab it and manage to spin in time to catch the axe with it. Another one moves in the corner of my eye, joining the one with the cleaver. Four total? That's about how many I heard.

"What the hell do you want?" I ask, trying to sound more angry than scared as I move with axe-guy, trying to keep all four in my view, but the one who no longer has a machete is already trying to get behind me.

"Don't pretend you don't know," the fourth guy says. He sounds young. Barely out of his teens. He's only a little younger than my son would be now. I shove that down. If he's trying to kill me, I can't think of him that way. "We saw you go into the blood bank. Looking like that."

"I'm a fucking vampire hunter!"

"Uh," the guy with the axe says helpfully.

"No," cleaver guy says.

I look between the four of them, narrowing my eyes. That bought me a few seconds, but if I don't convince them quickly, I'm likely to die by the hands of people who are supposed to be on the same side as me. I shift the machete to my left hand, moving my right slowly behind me. "If I wasn't a vampire hunter, would I have this?" I reach into the sheath secured to the small of my back and draw out my own machete. "You know many people who walk around with these under their jackets?"

The kid gulps, his eyes widening. "But…we saw you. Why would a vampire hunter go into the blood bank?"

"Gee, I dunno," I say, glaring at him. Now I'm regretting the comparison. This kid is an idiot. "Why were you watching it? It's almost like I'm trying to figure out where vampires would be since Toronto seems to be rather strange there."

Cleaver chuckles. "You expect me to believe that you don't know anything about this city? I know the hunters here, none of them look like you, and they sure as hell wouldn't be stupid enough to go ask around a blood bank."

"I'm not from around here."

He laughs more, stepping toward me. Axe finally lowers his weapon, at least, so I have two hands free if the three nearest attack. That's probably enough. "I can see that," he says. "And where might you be from?"

"Well, I cleared out Toledo before coming here. You have any friends down there? I'm sure they can verify me." I hope they don't call that bluff. I did, in fact, clear it out, but other hunters and I have never exactly gotten along well. It tends to go about like this. "I was in Lansing before then. I took care of all the leeches there as well."

"Bullshit," the kid says, spitting on the ground. "No one's that good."

I smirk but don't say anything else.

"You want us to believe that you go around clearing cities of vampires?" Cleaver asks.

I shrug, trying to seem as casual as I can when I'm outnumbered. "I don't particularly care if you believe it, but it's the truth. What I do care about is that you put your damn weapons down. I'm not your enemy. I don't have to be your friend, but if we could all walk away without any of us dying, I'd much prefer that."

Cleaver chortles, strafing around me, his hand still on the knife. He doesn't look jovial enough to be laughing this much. It worries me. What does he know that I don't? "How would a big-shot vampire hunter like you're pretending to be come to *Toronto* and not know shit about how it works?"

"I'm hunting a particular vampire." He's getting closer, and former-Machete is behind me. If they act, I don't think I can get away, at least not without killing them all, and I'd rather not take those odds. "I found out he moved to Toronto a while back. I intend to kill him, and I was going to kill the rest of the leeches in this town while I was at it, but if you'd prefer, I can only go after him. You want the rest to yourself?"

His laugh sounds more genuine, and he's close enough that I could take his arm with a machete. His arms are longer, so even with the cleaver, he can probably do the same. "Who's this vampire you're after?"

"I have a photo, but I have to reach in my pocket to get it, and I'm currently holding two machetes. If we'd all like to sheathe our weapons, I'll happily show you. Otherwise, I prefer to stay armed when there are three of you getting ready to attack one lone woman."

He stops mid-step, narrowing his eyes. It's a good trick. The kind of men who go into this line of work tend to be a bit old-fashioned. It's rarely done me any favors, but sometimes, misogyny can be exploited. "See, I don't think you're a woman. I think you're a monster."

"If I was a monster, why would I be talking? You've fought vampires, I assume?" A smile pulls at my cheeks, and I have to keep from snickering as I realize that I might be wrong. These guys could be so cautious because they haven't fought before. Vampires are strangely hard to find in Toronto, so maybe they never managed. If so, they'll probably play the part all the more, so it shouldn't affect anything. "You know how fast they are. How strong." I lightly shift the machetes, showing their weight and their sharpness. "If I was a vampire, you'd all be dead. This wouldn't be a conversation."

"I…"

"Yeah, right," the kid snaps. He looks terrified. I bet I could take a step, and he'd run away. That would leave three. I could handle three in a pinch. But I'd rather not take the risk.

"You're not…" Cleaver sighs, sucking on his cheek.

Axe stares at him. "She's a vampire. Look at her, she has to be."

He sheathes the cleaver at his hip. "Put your weapons down," he says. "Let's talk this out."

"You're joking!" the kid shouts.

I sheathe my machete, still holding the one in my left hand. I don't have a sheath for it, so this could get awkward.

Axe glares hard at me, hefting his axe, seeming to weigh the decision, but he drops it into its holster on his belt.

The guy behind me steps closer, and I spin around, but I don't swing. That could start a chain reaction.

"Can I have my machete back?"

I look between him and it, trying to decide. It's nice having a backup. They break rather easily in spines. I flip it so I'm gripping the blade and hold it out. "Sure. Just don't go using it on me."

He snatches it, stepping away, holding it at the ready until he's a few paces away, when he finally sheathes it. "Thanks," he mutters.

"So who's this vampire?" Cleaver says behind me.

I turn, pulling out the picture and point him out, my finger tapping his blond hair. He takes the picture, and I bite my tongue, clenching my fist. He doesn't trust me, and I'm not inclined to trust him. I don't like handing it over like this. It's one of the only leads I've ever managed to find. If he keeps it…I won't allow him to keep it.

"And why are you after him?"

I gulp. Probably not the best group of people to come out to. "He killed my family."

He nods and hands the picture back.

I let out a sigh of relief as I take it.

"A lot of us have stories like that," he says, sounding more somber.

I nod. From the handful of vampire hunters I've known, it seems nearly all of us lost a loved one. What else would send someone out into this life? "Have you seen him? Do you know anything about him?"

He shakes his head. "I'm afraid not. Everybody, take a look."

I hold it out, letting the other two adults see it, but they both shake their heads. Finally, the kid walks up to me, still eyeing me suspiciously. "I still don't trust you," he says.

"I don't trust you either."

That seems to take him aback. He hesitates and finally looks at the picture. "I don't know him."

"That's about what I figured. Well, with that covered, I do have another question, what is it that makes Toronto so strange? Why aren't there more vampires?"

Cleaver sighs. "I'm not sure you'll believe us."

"There's blood delivery." I look around, trying to find where the paper flew off to. "After that, I'll believe almost anything."

"They have a centralized society. From the sounds of it, commerce and everything, but I've never known anyone who got close and made it back alive. I'm not sure where it is."

I stare at him, tilting my head. That doesn't make any sense. "What?"

"Like I said, you wouldn't believe us."

"No. That's...what vampires manage a society? They're parasites. They couldn't."

He nods. "That's what I said when I got here. But it's true. And it's not only vampires. All kinds of creatures you can't even imagine live here, co-mingling in some fucked-up little mockery of society."

"Bullshit."

He chuckles. "Just you wait and see. I think it's Etobicoke now, but that's all I know. The few hunters I knew who investigated around there in the last few years, I haven't seen them since."

"Thank you." I'll have to look up where Etobicoke is, but it's the biggest lead I've had so far. Other than maybe that delivery place. I still need to start there, especially if the fatality rate in Etobicoke is that high. I'd rather go with the safer option first.

Axe smacks my shoulder. "Oh, don't thank us. I still think you're a vampire, so if you go to Etobicoke and come back alive, well, that proves me right."

"Or it proves that I'm as good as I say."

"Right," the kid mutters, sounding a tad incredulous. "No one clears a town of vampires. We're gonna be keeping an eye on you."

Cleaver glances at him, but rather than reprimanding him, he nods. He sucks on his teeth as he turns back to me, meeting my eyes. "I'd like to think that you're what you say you are, and you didn't kill me, which I do appreciate. If I hear anything about your vampire, I'll let you know."

"How will you contact me?"

"We'll be in touch," he says, matter-of-factly. "But if I find out that you're one of them, you won't have the chance to act. I will end you."

"Good to know." Now this is about how it normally ends. That's more like it.

He waves to his comrades. "We'll leave you to your investigation. Don't forget, we're watching you."

I grab my phone from the ground and find it cracked. When I press the lock button, the screen doesn't come on. Great. I scan the parking lot and finally locate the paper. I'll have to get a new phone and call them in the morning. It's getting close to midnight, and I doubt any store is open.

I stare at the door to the hospital. Why is the blood bank still open? I hadn't thought about it before I went in. Maybe they work with the delivery company? Or maybe those are normal hours here.

It can wait. I need sleep and a phone.

The former will have to come first.

CHAPTER THREE

I sit up, panting, clutching my face. The gold chain of my necklace feels cool against my burning skin. I can still smell the fire. I know that's not what happened. There wasn't a fire. It's not how they died. It wasn't my fault.

Rashad's hand is still in mine, clutching me. I look, and it's gone.

I rub my temple, trying to steady my breathing.

They're normally not that bad.

I climb out of bed, trying not to dwell on it but unable to see anything else. It didn't burn, not until a year later when a bomb fell on it. They were long dead. And it wasn't my fault. I know that. I was there. I saw it.

Tears well up, and I run to the bathroom to splash them away. I don't have time to live in the past.

I'm closer than I've ever been. Reynolds is in Toronto. Or at least, he was. He'll pay. That's all that can matter.

And I'll kill every fucking leech between him and me.

I shower and throw on clean clothes before heading to the store and grabbing a new prepaid phone. I stare at it in its packaging and look to the cash register. I don't have a choice. I can't continue my investigation without it. But after this, I'll be left with fifty bucks in cash and maybe a cup of coffee in my bank account after the hotel charges, if I'm being generous.

I let the cashier scan it and pay, watching my funds deplete. Vampire hunting is tragically not a well-paying profession. I make most of my money in poker or pool. With fifty dollars, I'll be lucky to manage that.

At least I'm already in the right town. Once I find him, it won't matter anymore. Once he's gone, I can finally rest.

I chuckle as I get back in my truck, which would probably get me about a grand if I sold it, so not worth it. There's no way I'd ever stop doing this. I've spent eighteen years doing nothing but hunting vampires. I could chop off that bastard's head tonight, and I'd probably be hunting the next day. I know myself better than to think it will ever end.

Though I would appreciate it if he had some cash in his pockets so I wouldn't have to worry about how I was going to afford gas.

Food isn't even a possibility. I sigh.

And that means I can't afford to order the stupid blood delivery. I slam my head against the back of the seat. How didn't I think of that earlier? I could've done something last night instead of going straight to bed. I could have robbed a damn bank. At least then I'd be able to afford to continue my investigation.

I still have the fifty dollars. I can use that.

But then I can't make any money. If I don't have anything to bet, I can't earn more, and it isn't like I have a line of credit I can draw from. I haven't had a real job since I came to the US, let alone to Canada. My parents would be so proud of what I'm doing with my doctorate.

Windsor is four hours away. I can't believe I was too dumb to stop at a casino on the way. I normally do backroom games and tend to avoid anyplace that might have security wanting to hassle me for winning too much. But the real reason I skipped it is because I was too bent on getting to town and killing him. Now I've been here for days, and I'm not any closer, and I'm broke. If I'd been smart, I'd have enough left to grease some palms and find out where he is, but instead, I'm stuck without enough gas to drive back to the casino if I want to still have money left to gamble.

I shouldn't have booked the whole week at once. Now I can't check out to have some gambling money.

"Fuck it," I mutter. I'll call the place, and I can rob the driver. I won't even need to give him money in the first place. He's delivering blood to monsters; it's not like he has much of a moral high ground, so there's no reason not to kill him. I grab the flyer from my glove compartment and dial the number. It rings. And rings. And keeps ringing.

I stare at my phone, but it doesn't make it stop ringing. I doublecheck the number, but it matches the flyer, so I hang up and try again.

It keeps ringing without an answer. I let it go for several minutes, tapping my fingers impatiently on the steering wheel. Nothing.

No answer at all.

It's like they don't want my money. Or to be killed and have their clientele list stolen, but they don't know that part.

I try one more time. Still nothing.

Are they closed? It's a little past noon, so it's possible that they're only open at night, but too many vampires don't mind the sun for that to make sense. I stare at the flyer. I want to crumple it up and throw it, but it's the only solid lead I've found so far, and tossing it aside seems like a waste.

Could the number be wrong? Would they have misprinted it and not noticed? What could I even do to find the right number? Try changing out some of the digits? None of them seemed misprinted.

I groan. It's probably not worth it. I have to assume that the number on the flyer is correct, and that there's some other reason they're not answering. What I should do is find out who owns the number.

I google it, finding that it's local. I have a membership to one of those number tracking websites that I will have to remember to cancel soon if I don't want an overdraft fee. An Etobicoke landline. Didn't those hunters tell me about that town? This is certainly adding up.

Maria Paulson is the name listed as the owner. Her first address is a good half hour away, but I don't have anything better to do. She has a few other numbers I could try first, though. Grinding my teeth, I stare at them and then at the road. If I call and she decides it's too suspicious, she could run before I get there, but if I manage to order a delivery, I'm a lot more likely to be able to get at least a few addresses rather than risking her burning them all.

It's risky, but I want to go with the option that doesn't mean waiting around for a delivery. I need to do something to feel like I'm actually making progress.

I start the truck, much to its protestations, and pull onto the road, heading for Etobicoke.

❖

The first address is a normal house. It's a little on the small side and has a child's bike and a few toys in the yard. "Shit."

I watch the house for any signs of movement. Will the kids be at school? How old are they? Are they even human?

"Fuck," I add for good measure, running my fingers through my hair, trying to think of what to do. If it was only vampires, I could go in, kill them all, and find any information they have on their buyers, then be out hunting the leeches before anyone could start to grow suspicious. But I can't do that in front of a kid.

I park in front of a nearby house, turn off the engine, and watch. No one seems to be moving inside, and the lights are off. I give it another ten minutes, and still, no one seems to be there.

I get out, trying to avoid looking around as I walk straight to the house and around to the backyard. It's fenced in, and there's a dog who starts barking the second he sees me. I glance around for anything I can throw. This golden retriever is clearly not a guard dog since it looks a lot more like he wants to play than take a bite of me, but he could attract attention either way.

The yard has a swing set, a tree house, and eight toys all covered in chew marks, but on my side of the fence, I see a few trees and some littered chip bags. I grab a branch from a nearby tree and head to the gate. I hope this works.

I throw the stick and open the gate, closing it behind me to not let the dog out. He chases the stick, completely ignoring me.

The back door is locked, but I have picks in my jacket pocket, so I get to work.

The dog starts licking my hand as I try. "I kinda need to concentrate."

He looks at me and switches to licking my face. I try to ignore it the best I can as I get the last tumbler in place. I stand, patting the dog on his head. "Thanks for not eating me."

He wags.

"I'm pretty sure you're supposed to stay out here." I open the door, and he runs right inside. "No! No, no, no!" I chase him, grabbing him by the collar and getting a pitiful whimper in return as I drag him back to the door and close it behind him.

As an alarm goes off.

"Great." I take in a deep breath, letting it out slowly. Police response is likely to be about five minutes minimum, if they actually respond. The phone will be ringing off the hook soon, but it's better to leave it unanswered.

I look through the house. On the first floor, there's an upscale kitchen, a living room with a massive TV, a playroom full of toys and games, and a den with a computer in it. I nudge the mouse, and the screen lights up to demand a password. I try "password" and "123456," but neither work, so I glance around for a sticky note. The phone on the desk starts ringing, but I ignore it, pulling open a drawer.

And can't help but grin when I find exactly what I'm looking for. The password is two names and a birth date. Twins? That's adorable. I log in as Maria—so this is her place—and take a look through the documents folder. None of the titles stand out. Taxes, presentation3, and other similar file names don't give anything away, so I open the first three and wait for the computer to respond. It's faster than I'd feared, but there's still a considerable delay for each file.

Normal taxes, more taxes, family vacation collage, stock info, and a list of names with addresses and credit cards.

I hit print on the list and close out of everything before locking the computer. I don't have time to investigate further. I just have to hope this is it. It sure looks it.

How many pages is this thing? It keeps printing.

I tap my foot, staring at the phone as it rings again. Is this the one I tried to call? It ends, doubtless going to voice mail, so it couldn't be the one I was calling.

To test that theory, I try calling the number again. It rings in my ear, and the phone on the desk stays silent. Then starts ringing.

I hang up, and it keeps going, so the two are unrelated.

Five pages now, and it's still going. I check on the printer's display, see that it's twenty-three pages, and cancel the print order before snatching the papers it already printed and heading out the back door.

The dog tries to run inside again, but I close the door in time and jump over the fence to avoid letting him out. He's a kid's dog, and I'm not willing to let them lose him. And it would prove that someone was there.

No cops are waiting by my truck, so I get in and drive away, hoping no one took down my license while I was in there.

Once I'm a few miles away, I pull into the parking lot of a gas station and look over the pages. His name isn't on it. I should've searched the document, but I figured I'd have time to do it after I left.

How am I going to figure out if this list is legitimate? The name on the computer at least matched the one for the number I called, so unless the flyer is outdated, that's a good sign, but for all I know, this could be the client info for some innocent lady's Etsy shop.

She didn't even have a password protecting the file, despite it having credit card numbers. That's not exactly professional level.

I could either start going down the list and see if the people are actually people, or I could investigate Maria's other address.

I wanted to be thorough. And if she realizes someone broke into her house, she'll probably step up the security for anyplace else, so it's smart to act quickly.

Hopefully, she won't warn her clients. She won't want them thinking they can't trust her, and what are a few dead monsters to her business's integrity?

I drive over to the other address, only a few miles from her house.

I stare at it, my mouth going dry. It's a clinic.

The sign proudly reads Etobicoke Family Medical Clinic. She's harvesting from people seeing her for treatment and using it to feed these leeches. I thought medical care had advanced since those days. I want to laugh at the joke, but I can't. She's betraying these people's trust to feed monsters. Even if she's human, that makes her a monster, even worse than the ones she's feeding them to. She deserves to die.

And she's using it to provide for her kids.

It isn't an excuse. But how can I kill someone who's only providing for their children? This is enough evidence. It proves she's doing it by feeding innocent people to monsters. I know that she's the one selling blood, and that this client list is likely what I'm looking for. I don't need to go in and talk to her. I don't want to kill a kid's mother, and I'm not sure I'd be able to stop myself from doing it then and there with the way she treats the very people she's supposed to be caring for.

She better not be doing the same to her kids, or else I will be meeting her.

I drive away, heading to the first name on the list. It's time to meet Phillip Anderson.

CHAPTER FOUR

I pull to a stop in front of a run-down building. The whole neighborhood looks like it's waiting to be demolished, but the address on the list is the worst of them. There's no way anyone's living in it. It looks almost as bad as my apartment did after the bombing. I've seen vampires nest in worse but not by much.

I approach the building, and a wretched stench fills my lungs. Dead bodies. Several of them.

I cover my mouth, trying not to think about it as I approach the front door, and the scent grows overpowering. They're not fresh. They must've been rotting for days. I let out a breath, trying not to inhale as I open the door. It doesn't quite fall off its hinges, but it's hanging on by a thread as it swings open.

If the scent was overwhelming outside, I can't even begin to describe it this close. It almost knocks me off my feet. Urine, feces, decay, and something else that I can't quite place and don't want to. Trying not to vomit, I look through the building.

It doesn't take long to find the first body. They're sitting at the dining room table with a tourniquet around their arm. I don't see a needle, but their throat has a gash from where a vampire must've pulled away, satisfied.

I close my eyes, trying not to see the image, but the one in my head is worse. My wife, her eyes growing faint, her throat as torn as this man's. I force them open and step away, only keeping from hurling because I don't have anything to throw up.

There are two more bodies down here, but I can't bear to look at them. I take the stairs, the second step breaking under my foot, and the banister snapping and falling to the ground when I try to catch myself. I press against the wall and stay on my feet, keeping to the side of the stairs as I move to the second floor. The place is falling apart. I've been in places in better condition after they were hit by a bomb.

Another body lies in the hallway, his eyes closed.

He looks fresher.

I move closer and risk an inhalation. The scent of decay still fills my lungs, but it's not coming from this man. He smells dead but without the rot or emptiness of a real corpse.

He's not any deader than other leeches; he's just high off his ass from the junkies he killed. I stare at the sleeping vampire. It will only take a second to slice his head off, but I can't waste a lead like this.

I draw my machete and hold it to his throat before kicking his hip.

The blade's sharp enough that his jostling causes it to dig in, drawing blood. He drank enough that he can bleed from a nick? I can barely resist shoving it forward until it carves right to the floor. "Wha—"

"Shut up," I say. "One word I don't like and you see how sharp this is."

"Who—"

"That's not a word I like, but you have one more chance. I'm not here to answer your questions. I'm going to show you a photo. I want you to look real hard, through all that heroin, and tell me if you know the person in it. If you're honest, you get to live."

He gulps. There's nothing like seeing fear in the eyes of a predator. This man…this creature killed those people without a second thought, and now he's scared. Of me. It's intoxicating.

I fish in my pocket with my free hand and pull out the photo. "Do you know this man?" I tap where he is. I know this picture like the back of my hand, and I can pinpoint the monster who killed my family with my eyes closed.

His eyes widen.

"The one with his shirt open. The blond. Do you know him?"

He keeps staring but very slowly shakes his head.

"You're sure?"

He nods.

I take the photo back. "Thank you for being honest." I cleave his head from his neck, then jump down the rotting stairs and out to my truck. One down, thirty-seven to go, thirty-eight if I can grab the address from the phone number of the cutoff entry from when I had to cancel the print.

The second name on the list is in an apartment building that seems normal. The leech must be preying on their neighbors. I pick the lock and close the door behind me, but the place is empty. There's a bed, a TV, a phone charger, some clothes, and that's it. There's not even a computer.

I fish through the pockets of the jackets and find a twenty. My lucky day. I put it in my wallet and finish my search. Nothing. I'll come back later.

I lock the door and head back to my truck, glancing over my list. The third name is Crocetti, Olivia. Hopefully, this one goes better. The address isn't another dilapidated building waiting for demolition or even a nice apartment. It's an actual mansion. I stare at it. The leech has a damn manor. Who the hell did she steal that from?

In my eighteen years hunting these things, I've never seen one live in a mansion. This isn't *Dracula*. Why would a leech pay for this kind of place? I stare at the private road, well removed from the main street, and think of a reason: no neighbors to call the police when the victims start screaming.

There's a standalone garage with its door closed, so I pull in front of it. It'll keep Olivia from leaving too easily. I go around the side and pick the lock on the garage door. Two cars inside. Does that mean there's more than one of these creatures here?

I move to the front door, pick the lock, and pull it open. I take a few steps in, and an alarm starts blaring.

What vampire has a security system? I'm insulted. Why would they ever involve the cops?

They wouldn't. They can't have legal citizenship papers if they're older than a few decades, and this Olivia must be far older to save up for this kind of place.

The alarm keeps blaring from a room to the right. Why wouldn't it be by the door?

I go in and turn the light on, hoping to find the source of the alarm, only to turn it back off, then on again—because clearly, I can't manage to act professional when it could get me killed—and again, only to find a birdcage with a blanket over it. The siren is coming from under the blanket.

I lift it up and find a parrot screaming at me.

"Who the hell are you?"

That doesn't come from the parrot. At least, not at first. It repeats it as I turn and find a tall woman with dreadlocks, in her pajamas, holding a sword.

"You must be Olivia," I say, trying not to let the fear show. She's already armed, and my machete is still under my jacket. There's absolutely no way I can draw and swing faster than a vampire can strike. She can kill me before I move. All I can do is act like I know something she doesn't and hope it's enough to buy time, and that with said time, I can get my weapon out without losing an arm.

She takes a step back. That's unexpected. "What? How do you know my name?" Her sword trembles, and her voice quakes as she speaks.

Why is she scared? She is a vampire, isn't she? "I don't think that matters much," I say. "The point is, I know what you are. Vampire."

Her back presses against the wall with the light switch. "You…" She doesn't manage any more.

I have no idea what's going on, but I draw my weapon. Her eyes widen as she stares at the machete, shaking all the harder.

Normally, I quite enjoy killing vampires. It's almost like sex. But this is rubbing me the wrong way. She's looking at me like I'm some kind of monster when she's the murderous leech.

I step toward her, trying to steel my expression and not let her see the confusion and guilt as I bare my machete threateningly.

She squeaks.

"What the hell?" I ask.

She doesn't say a word.

"You are a vampire, right?"

Nothing.

I stare, pulling my machete back, ready to swing, but I can't do it. She's cowering from me, and I'm not sure she's a vampire. She's a little on the pale side for a black woman but not enough for me to say for sure, and I've never seen a vampire shake and…and now there are tears in her eyes.

No, she's trying to trick me. But why? I need to kill her already. This is ridiculous. But I can't kill a crying woman. I shake my head, trying to avoid seeing the dying crying woman I always see when I close my eyes. "You're a monster. A murderer," I say, trying to sound like I believe it.

"Stay the hell away from her," another voice shouts. It's not the parrot. Someone dashes through the doorway, crashing into me like a semitruck. Probably harder.

I slam into the wall. Plaster and wood crumble around me as I stare at the woman who hit me. I feel my chest and find that it gives far too easily. She broke a few ribs. More like shattered, by the feel of it. It's not that bad. It should only hurt too much if I breathe.

I blink and shake my head. My machete is still in my hand. The woman who tackled me is wearing a bathrobe, and her fangs are showing. At least now I know this one is definitely a vampire. Maybe this is Olivia? I try not to breathe to avoid my ribs stabbing my lungs.

"You're still alive. How? I was worried I'd killed someone but just…" She trails off and looks to the panicked woman. "Are you okay, Ollie?"

So the black one *is* Olivia.

The cowering woman looks between her and me. "You're...
not a hunter?" She gulps again and takes a deep breath.

I start to reply, but the vampire with no name knocked all the
air out of my lungs, so I don't have anything to form words with. I
take a shallow breath. "I am."

She narrows her eyes, gripping the sword tighter. "You're a
vampire."

I snarl. "I'm nothing like you!"

"I broke at least three of your ribs and hit you hard enough
that a concussion should be the least of your worries," the other
woman says. "You're not human."

I test out my arms. Neither are broken. I take a step, and my
legs handle me fine. I can still kill them. The pain with every step
is just a minor nuisance. I rush the one who attacked me, but Olivia
swings for my arm, and I have to leap back to avoid her, only for
the other one to charge me. I slash at her throat, and Olivia parries.
They're trying to protect each other? That's unusual.

"I can take care of her, Mia." Olivia says. She looks very
different from the terrified woman huddled against the wall from
a few minutes ago. If I didn't know better, I'd say she looks like a
soldier. "Go back to bed."

"You were cowering from me a minute ago. What the hell is
going on?" I've never seen a vampire act like this before, but it
won't keep me from killing her.

The other one, Mia, rolls her eyes. "You break into our house
to kill us and have the nerve to ask questions?"

"Please, I don't want you to have to see this," Olivia says.

"Stay," I spit, wincing from the pain in my chest. "I can kill
you both."

Mia kicks, and I swing to slice her leg off, but Olivia parries
my strike again, and I have to shove off her weapon to get the
space between us. "You're a vampire that hunts vampires? I think
I've seen that movie."

"I'm not a vampire." I rush her again, but I know what to expect this time, so when Olivia moves in, I sweep her leg out from under her and grab her sword as she goes to the floor, but I have to back away when Mia comes to her rescue. Vampires don't care about each other. They're merciless creatures that want nothing but murder. What the hell is going on?

"If you're not a vampire, why isn't your heart beating?" Mia asks.

She's trying to take me off-balance, but I now have both the weapons in this fight. She can't get under my skin. "I might be dead, but it doesn't make me like you. I don't prey on the innocent. I'm not a monster."

"You do know you're a vampire, then, and you're simply trying to justify it."

I swing at her with Olivia's sword, but Olivia grabs my wrist and wrenches it back. Hard.

The bone snaps through the skin, but it doesn't pierce my jacket. My vision goes white for a second, but I shake it off. It's not important. I can still fight. A couple drops of blood fall to the floor, but that's it. I suppose there's not much left in me.

Mia covers her mouth and looks nauseous.

"I told you I didn't want you to see this," Olivia says. "She's a vampire. I can handle vampires."

"Didn't stop me from having to save you last time."

Olivia shoots her a glare. A point of contention? Can I use that to gain the upper hand? I try to say something but can only manage a pained grunt. It's only an arm. And a few ribs. I can still win. I can still kill these wretched leeches.

"That was different," Olivia says. "Please. You know you don't have the stomach for this."

"I'm a surgeon, I do worse all the time." Mia doesn't sound convincing.

I lunge for Olivia with the machete, but she moves to grab it again, so I feint and take both of her arms, the blade slicing clean through the bones and sending her hands falling to the floor with a meager spray of blood. The fight's almost mine. Before I can go in for the kill, Mia tackles me, knocking me to the ground and sending the machete skittering on the floor. She slams her fist into my face. "You monster!"

I try to block, but my broken arm doesn't cooperate. I must be in agony but I can hardly even feel it. I just know that my arm is refusing to budge. I try to force it to move. It broke at the elbow. I should still be able to use my shoulder.

Her fist slams into my jaw hard enough that I feel it crack. It's barely more than a gentle hum under the rest of the pain.

Blocking is a waste of time. I slug her back with enough force that she rocks off me for an instant. I roll, grabbing her by her throat and taking her with me, pressing down. It'll be hard to take her head off like this. "You're the monster." I sound like a whining child. It's pathetic. I've been through so much worse than this.

She scratches at my hand, but she doesn't have much in the way of nails.

"You're a killer. A leech. I'll make sure you can't hurt anyone again."

Something hits me from behind and sends me tumbling into the wall. An armless Olivia, bleeding a lot more than I am, stares me down. "The only monster I see here is you," she says.

"You should check a mirror." The words pulse through the crack in my jaw. I should probably shut up if I don't want it to actually split open. But I can hardly ignore their slander. I won't stand here and be insulted by vampires.

She smirks, and I wonder if she can see herself in mirrors. I've only seen a couple vampires who didn't have reflections, but it made those hunts quick and easy, even if I did have to hurry out of that bar before anyone checked the restroom. "You break into people's houses and murder them. She's a doctor, and the only person she's ever killed was a centuries-old, racist, serial killer."

I stare at her, rubbing my jaw. "Why the hell would I believe a vampire?" My jaw clicks when I speak. That's not a great sign.

Mia climbs to her feet, looking between us. "How are you alive if you don't know you're a vampire too?"

"I know what I am." I clench my fist, trying to weigh my odds. They're both injured, especially Olivia, the better fighter. If I can get my good hand on the sword or the machete, I still might be able to win. I'm not leaving here without their heads. All vampires do is hurt people. I couldn't live with myself if I let these monsters keep doing so.

The weapons are both by Olivia's feet. Mia is to the side but between us. My back is almost to the wall. There's a window with the curtain drawn next to a big crack from where I was tackled before. I could rush for the window and hope one of them is weak to the sun, but if they're not, then I'm dead.

"A vampire," Mia says. "You can say it." She sounds somewhere between taunting and therapeutic.

She's trying to rattle me, not help me. I won't let her get to me. I'm not that dumb.

"Or a leech. That's what you called me, isn't it? That's considered a slur, by the way." She laughs, and it's so insulting that I want to hit her. "But you're the same as we are."

Olivia rolls her eyes, unable to do much more. That at least gives me some comfort.

"Fine," I snap. "I'm a..." I try to force myself to say it, to prove that it doesn't bother me, that she's not getting to me. But I can't say the word.

"Vampire," she says.

I rush her and get kicked right in the head, adding a ringing to the collection of sensations rolling around there. I stumble back, trying to grab something to keep me on my feet. I grab the drapes, but it's not enough, and I still end up on my ass, ripping them from the window.

Someone screams, and I pull myself free to find them both gone.

What the hell? Why wouldn't they take the chance to finish me off? Are they that weak to the sun?

I should leave. I should be smart and walk right out of here. I can head right back into the sunny day that I came from. I'm in no condition to continue the fight

But one of them was screaming in pain, and they both ran away. The sun did half my job for me. I can't leave and give them time to eat some innocent victim and recover. I pick up my machete and head farther into the house, the bird squawking after me.

They're not in the foyer or in the living room right by me, so I head farther in and find an impressively spacious kitchen with a burnt body standing in front of the fridge. It's clawing at it, desperately, and letting out something that I could vaguely still call a pained cry. "Holy fuck," I mutter.

Olivia is next to her, looking helpless.

I move toward them, ready to take them out of my misery, and I suppose theirs.

"Please," Olivia says.

I hesitate.

She's not kicking me. That's strange. I don't like it.

The burnt body collapses. It has to be Mia. I've never seen anyone this sensitive to the sun before.

"You didn't kill me when I was having a panic attack," Olivia said. "Clearly you're not a complete monster. Please. She's never hurt anyone who didn't deserve it. She's never even attacked a human. Please, just get her the blood from the fridge." Each sentence sounds more panicked than the last. She's being genuine. What the hell vampire actually cares enough about someone to be this frantic?

I look between them.

"You can kill me after." It's a trick. It has to be. Vampires don't care about others. They're nothing but soulless monsters bent on killing.

And yet she's offering her life in exchange for this vampire. This woman. Just like I tried to. She must love her; it's the only possible explanation, even if it means vampires are capable of such a thing. "Fuck, fine!" I throw my machete, burying it in the kitchen wall, and yank the fridge open. The door hits Mia's leg and earns a pained whimper. The fridge is mostly full of vegetables, but there are several bags of blood on the bottom shelf, so I grab one, rip it open, and hold it to her mouth. I'm feeding a vampire. I should be killing her.

At first, it looks like she can't manage to drink, but it pours onto her lips, and she manages a few gulps. Her face starts to look more human, and she snatches the bag, sucking on it like on a juice box.

It's disgusting. It's still blood. She's still a monster. I shouldn't be saving her. What the hell is wrong with me?

"Thank you," Olivia says.

"Fuck you."

She snorts. "Have you never met another vampire who doesn't kill?"

"I'm not...you're all monsters."

"*We're* all monsters, you mean."

I glare at her and glance toward my machete, its hilt protruding from the wall.

"I *am* a monster, if that makes you feel any better. And I suspect you are, as well. But she's not, and she doesn't deserve to be hunted. You lot, vampire hunters, nearly hunted us all to extinction. I was there for it. People I loved murdered other people I loved because some asshole wrote a book. Humans are monsters, and they don't have the excuse of needing to feed."

"They killed you...they killed us because we hunt them."

I have the distinct impression she would be crossing her arms if she had any. "You don't know what it was like."

"I do know what it's like to have a vampire murder everyone I love."

Is that guilt on Olivia's face? It fades as quickly as it appeared, but I swear she looked stricken. "And how many loved ones have you killed?"

"I only kill monsters. No one loves monsters."

"And innocent vampires who've never harmed a soul, who didn't deserve it? Like Mia?"

I look down at Mia. She's panting and looks almost human. "Is that true?"

She nods and stares at the empty blood bag.

"She needs more," Olivia says.

"You said give her the one, and I can kill you."

She stretches out her neck. "Fine. Then do it. If that's what you want, kill me. I don't stand a chance at this point."

I look to my machete, still buried in the wall, knowing she'll attack if I turn to get it, but when I look back, she hasn't moved an inch. She's just standing there, waiting.

Mia tries to pull herself to her feet, but she's clearly too weak. I could kill them both right now. I wouldn't lose any sleep. They're monsters.

I could walk right out if she didn't look so helpless. "Watch your feet," I mutter and open the fridge.

CHAPTER FIVE

W hat's your name?" Mia is sitting on the kitchen counter, looking as human as a vampire can, sipping blood out of a cup and studying me.

I stare at my own cup of warm blood. I feel sick. No one has ever watched me drink before, let alone two leeches. Now that the fight's over, I can feel the bone sticking out of my arm and how pulverized my ribs are. The pain is barely enough to get me to give in to the craving. I take a sip of the blood. It's so revolting, drinking this shit. It's delicious.

I gulp it, feeling my bones knit back together.

Olivia tests out her reattached arms, lifting her own half-empty cup. "You are a guest in our house. Now. You don't think the least you can do is say that much?"

I sigh. "It's Kalila."

"I'm Mia. You know, one of the people you were trying to kill."

"You're not a person."

"Then neither are you."

I shut up and drink my blood.

"Thank you," Olivia says, leaning against the counter by who I assume is her wife. "I'm Olivia, and if I was in your shoes, I don't know if I would have let us live. Vampires are almost as bad as humans."

"Humans are just our victims." I hate talking like this. It's not "us" or "our." It's them and me. I'm not like them. But how can I say that when Mia has a lower body count than I do? Even only counting humans.

"Why did you spare us?"

I shrug. "Maybe you remind me of my wife and I."

"You're married?" Mia asks. "I can't imagine anyone putting up with you. I've known you for half an hour, and I'd probably try to kill you again if I had the chance."

"Never legally. But yeah, I was. We had a son."

"Oh." She stares at her cup, apparently learning far too much from that answer. I hate being honest with people, but then again, they're not people. "I'm sorry. So that's why you—"

"Yeah." I don't want to hear anything she has to say on it. I pull out my photo and hold it out to Olivia. "Do either of you know this man? The blond one." I tap on him.

She leans in, studying the picture. "No. I don't. I assume he's the one who did it?"

"He is."

Turning to Mia, she asks, "Has he come into your clinic?"

She sucks her lower lip and takes the picture, holding it to her eyes. Finally, she shakes her head. "No. He's pretty nondescript, but I don't think I've ever seen him. He have a name? Maybe I'd recognize that."

She's actually a doctor. Is it only to get blood? What vampire treats people? "Gregory Reynolds."

"It doesn't ring a bell. I'm sorry. Genuinely. You're a monster, and I don't care if he kills you, but that doesn't mean your family deserved it."

"They didn't." I snatch the picture back, careful not to rip it. "Great. I followed him all the way to Toronto, and no one fucking knows a thing." It's only been a few days. I shouldn't be acting like this yet. But it's hard not to. At first, this city was so strange, and I couldn't even find vampires, and now that I have, I'm no closer. And I didn't kill two of the ones I met.

"How far back was this?" Mia asks. "Like, when did he come to Toronto?"

"About eighteen years ago. I finally found out and came after him from America, and no one here has heard of him. I'm starting to worry it was a bad lead."

"You could always ask around the Community Center."

I stare. What is that? They've been surprisingly accommodating for people I was trying to kill a few minutes ago. "What's the Community Center?"

"Wow, you are new around here," Olivia says. "It's where all the fiends shop."

"There's actually some sort of monster society here?"

"They prefer the term fiends if you don't want to be murdered right away."

"I'll kill them first."

Olivia looks between her blood and me. "A lot of them don't hurt people. And if you go to the Community Center, they have rules against fighting. You cause trouble, and you're not going to like the results."

"I've dealt with worse."

"Unless you've killed a few thousand vampires at once, no, you haven't. Normally, I'd be happy to see a vampire hunter get killed, but you're my guest, and you saved my wife's life, even if you are the one who nearly killed her in the first place. Keep your head down. It's at the old Honeydale Mall. I'm sure you can find it, and maybe you can get answers there."

A vampire is actually helping me. I don't like it. I finish the rest of my blood and rinse the cup in the sink. "I'm sorry. For trying to kill you." I should still kill them. I can't humanize them. They may look like us, like *them*, but it doesn't mean they are.

"You almost succeeded," Mia says, still not bothering to hide her anger.

I want to say, "Maybe next time." But she's an innocent victim. "You've really never killed a human?"

She shakes her head. "Never been too fond of humans. I'd rather not have to bite one. Having to drink blood is already gross enough. The only person I've killed was a vampire."

I stare at my machete, still in the wall. She's a vampire. She's a monster. Why doesn't she deserve it?

"Have you not drunk before?" Olivia asks. "You know what you're doing, so I assume you weren't recently turned."

I gulp, wishing I still had a drink and hating myself for it when I realize that drink was blood. "I've drunk before. I've even killed. But I've mostly bought from blood banks, and sometimes, a hunter goes after me, and things get out of control." I stare at the floor, hating that I'm being this open, that these monsters can see me like this. The face of that child flashes in my eyes. He was a hunter. I didn't kill him, but I could have. Did I? They all blend together. I'm a monster too. What would stop me from killing that child in self-defense and draining him dry? Would I be any different from Reynolds? I shake my head. I'm nothing like him.

"It happens," Olivia says. "You can't blame yourself for trying to live. Christ, I can't believe hunters go after their own." She crosses herself, wincing.

I stare at her but don't bother asking. That's between her and her god. "If they're any good at sniffing out vampires, they can generally tell what I am, and sometimes, they don't listen to reason."

Mia crosses her arms. "Sounds familiar."

I shrug. They can hate me all they want. "Thanks for the tip. And the...drink. I'm going to check it out, assuming you're not planning on telling them I'm coming."

Olivia shakes her head. "No one in particular I'd warn. Just don't give them a reason to kill you. Or do. You're still a vampire hunter."

"I am." I glare, half expecting her to cower again, but she doesn't.

"I'll see you to the door. I'm sure you can't blame me for wanting to make sure."

I nod. "Let me get my stuff." I pull the machete from the wall, holding it for a second, needing to use it, but I sheathe it. "I think I left my hat in your bird's room." I stare at the curtains on the ground when I get there. Olivia is already right behind me. "Want to help me hang these back up?"

She scoffs and shakes her head but takes up the other end. They're torn in a few spots, but we secure them on the rod, and they block out the sun well enough that it should be safe.

Neither of us seems to know what to say, so I pick up my hat, and she leads me to the door.

I could still kill her. She's not like Mia. She deserves it. I'm sure of it.

We stare at each other for a long moment before I open the door.

Finally, she says, "I had someone like that soldier you're hunting. I never quite had the strength to chase him myself, but now that he's gone, it does help. I sleep a lot easier knowing he's dead. I'm sure you will too."

I study her. She doesn't look concerned for me, more like she's saying what coffee she recommends from a particular café. I nod. "I'm certain I will. All I have to do is find him."

Neither of us bother saying good-bye as I climb into my truck and drive away. I'll look up where the Community Center is once I'm not on a vampire's property.

CHAPTER SIX

I have to stop for gas, so I look up where the mall is while I'm in line. It's twenty minutes from the gas station, so it won't be too bad of a drive, but I have absolutely no idea what I'm walking into. My machete has seen better days after that fight, but I'm not spending the money to replace it.

I hand the stolen twenty to the clerk and head back to my truck, not quite filling it up. It'll have to last me until I can find a poker table or a very rich vampire I can kill. Though I was with one of those a few minutes ago. I should've done it. Why did I let her live?

She is a leech. She admitted she's a monster. What could possibly have possessed me to leave her in one piece? I even helped fix her arms after I cut them off.

There was no reason to help her. There wasn't even a reason to help Mia. She may be innocent by vampire standards, but she is still a vampire. What was I thinking, leaving them both alive? I could have taken Olivia's head at the door and walked right back in to finish Mia. I'm sure they have some cash lying around, and then I wouldn't be in such dire straits, and Toronto would have two fewer monsters to feed on its people.

But I couldn't bring myself to do it. It had to be the way she said "please." A monster was begging me to help the woman she loved.

GENEVIEVE McCLUER

I close my eyes and slam the pump back into its holster hard enough to dent it. I begged. And it didn't get me shit. I guess at least I know I'm better than him, but that's not much comfort. If I can't be as heartless as him, how can I know I'll have it in me to finish the job? If I'm going to compromise my morals and let monsters live, then what's the point? I've spent eighteen years doing nothing but hunting these creatures, and then one looks at me the right way and begs for her wife's life, and I spare them both?

I'm getting soft. And I can't risk that, not if I want to actually make a difference. My life's work is to cut down these miserable leeches and that bastard most of all, and I'm starting to sympathize with them.

If I'm the hunter I claim to be, I should drive right back there and kill them both. And I know I won't. Maybe I just can't take another happily married couple from this world, even if the comparison makes me feel sick.

I climb into the cab, grit my teeth, and drive to Etobicoke. I need to kill something, to remind myself that that's still who I am and that I still have the follow-through to do it, but instead, I have to play nice and talk to monsters like they're people. Otherwise, I can't find him.

Someone flashes their brights behind me. I try turning mine on, but the sun's still up, and they keep flashing, so I pull to the side of the road, and they follow.

Cleaver walks up to my window. At least I know for sure that I didn't eat him now. I roll it down and look at him, trying to figure out what he could possibly want.

"You're in Etobicoke," he says.

"I noticed."

He crouches until he can meet my eyes. His are the same brown as his hair and as bushy as his mustache, and they look oddly concerned. Maybe I'm not the only one growing soft. "I told you we'd be watching you."

"See anything interesting?"

He snickers, nodding. "Yeah. Yeah, I'd say we did."

I don't gulp or react, but I'm certain I grip the steering wheel tighter. Did he see a living vampire letting me out of her house without a fight? There hadn't been a window in the kitchen, so he at least didn't see me drinking. "Do tell."

"I'm sure you know."

I quirk an eyebrow.

"You've been running all over town. You did good work on that smack house. I burnt it down after you left. We don't need any evidence or more people finding out about this shit. If we're not keeping them innocent, what's the point?"

I narrow my eyes, trying to figure out what he wants.

"You might be as good as you say. Was there a vampire at that mansion?"

The thought of him trying to take on Olivia and Mia is funny enough that I have to force myself not to laugh. "No, just an acquaintance. I was hoping she'd have some information, but I came up empty."

"Hm." He nods, looking over me and the sheet of paper on the passenger seat. "What's that list?"

"A clue I'm looking into. Why? Were you hoping to work together?"

He sucks on his teeth, meeting my eyes again, seeming to probe, as if he's looking for an answer to an unspoken question. "We've lost a lot of hunters around here. I don't know what you think you're doing getting this close, but I have to assume that you're trying to find where they're meeting up."

"And if I am?"

"Then you're probably going to die."

I've done that before. I shrug. "If this is what finally kills me, then I'll die"

He looks down the road, then at me, and slowly nods. "Do you know where it is?"

If I tell him, he'll get himself killed too. "I have a few ideas, but I was going to check abandoned buildings and hope I get lucky."

"On your own?"

I try to hide my fear. He wants to come with me. All that would do is make it harder to get answers and guarantee he dies, and I'm not willing to have another human's death on my hands. "I don't play nice with others."

"My brother, he tried to find this place too. It was a month back, and I haven't seen him since. He taught me everything I know, and Etobicoke was too dangerous for him. You're only a girl. You don't know what you're walking into."

I'm quite certain I'm older than him. "I'll be fine. I promise, if you follow me again tomorrow, you'll find me in one piece. But don't get yourself killed keeping an eye on me tonight."

"You're one to talk there."

"Are you suspicious of me or worried about me?"

He stuffs his hands in his pockets and looks me up and down. "Both."

"I haven't proven myself yet?"

"I don't trust too many people, let alone weird foreign women who brag about doing impossible things."

"You've seen me fight."

"You barely held your own against me and my boys. That doesn't mean you'd beat a pack of vampires."

I sigh. "I wasn't trying to kill you."

He snorts. "Suppose you weren't."

"Do you have any other warnings you want to give, or can I leave?"

He steps back and walks to his car, then climbs in, and it pulls out, driving away. Maybe he's actually taking my advice.

I drive straight for the Honeydale Mall and hope those vampires weren't lying to me.

❖

The mall looks run-down and abandoned from the outside. Did Olivia lie to me? I wouldn't put it past her. She is a vampire, after all.

I park in front of it. There are two cars there, and they look almost as beat-up as my truck. This may simply be a place where people dump cars they can't sell. It doesn't mean there's actually any sort of monster society inside.

After making sure my machete is still safely secured to the small of my back, I climb out of my truck and head toward the entrance.

The first thing that hits me is the smell. There's meat, pastries, wet fur, blood, foul odors I couldn't possibly name, and the general scent of a crowd mingling and sweating together. This is the place. I open the door and step past the outer facade to enter a massive market, with monsters moving from stand to stand, talking, bartering, and in general, reminding me a bit of home.

Except that they're not human. Everyone wandering about has horns, tusks, cloven hooves, fur, fangs, or something else distinguishing them as quite obviously monsters. I've never seen this many in the same place before. I'd seen vampires, fairies, a couple demons, and a few other things I'd never heard the names of, but this is something entirely else. It's a cacophony of monstrous forms in more shapes than I'd ever have thought possible. And they're living under everyone's noses, preying on them.

Every muscle in my body tenses for a fight. I want to grab my machete and start cutting. But I'm massively outnumbered, and I'd die in a matter of seconds. That's not something I can allow before I find him. I don't care about my life, but he's damn sure going to Jahannam with me.

I look around the bazaar, trying to keep calm. I'm surrounded by monsters, any of which I'd kill in a second any other day, and I have to let them live if I want information. I glance from one stall to another for any sort of clue. Where the hell do I start?

It's a market, and that means I need money if I want to find anything out. So there is only one logical place to start. I walk up to the nearest stand, a clothing shop with garments in all sorts of strange configurations for any number of limbs or unusual parts. I try to look at them appreciatively and not think about the monstrosity opposite me. He's a minuscule man covered in plants both growing out of him and worn as clothes. It seems ironic that someone who doesn't wear clothes would sell them, but perhaps that's why. I've never seen one before, but there aren't too many other creatures that look like Elokos, and they're well-known for feasting on humans. I've had quite a while to look up the creatures I'm most likely to run across, particularly those who prey on humans. I haven't done it as much as I should've, and I don't have the best memory for them, but it's a lot easier than learning types of stars, if for no other reason than they're a lot more likely to try to eat me.

My machete chafes at my back, and I itch to draw it, to stop this creature from feeding on innocent people. If I don't, it'll bewitch them and eat them in a single bite. But if I do, then I'll never be able to kill Reynolds.

"See anything you like?" he asks.

I take a deep breath, trying to keep my hand from shaking. I have to kill him. It's the only answer. Can I actually be so selfish as to put my own need for revenge over the lives this monster will take?

And what of the lives that Reynolds will take? And all the other monsters I'll kill before and after him?

But does that mean that I should allow these creatures to live simply so I can hope to do good in the future? It's cowardice! "Is there a casino here?"

His beady eyes look me up and down. If I was still human, he'd probably be considering the best way to eat me. "Are you certain I can't interest you in any of these fine wares first?"

"Maybe after I win some money."

He chuckles amicably. The monster thinks he's being friendly. It's disgusting. "Then I suppose I'll see you then." A clawed hand points to the side, and I somehow keep from lopping it off.

"There're a few tables for cards over there, in one of the old stores. It's easy to look past, and the door is often closed, but it's about midway down the wall. I'm not sure if anyone is playing right now."

"Thank you." I turn and leave without another word. My hand aches. I don't know if I can handle spending long in this place.

CHAPTER SEVEN

The room is lit with Christmas lights and lamps. They must have never replaced the lighting after the place was shut down. Where would monsters hire an electrician?

There are three card tables, but only one of them is in use. Two largely human-looking beings sit at a table with something big and purple, its massive horns protruding out of its head. An oni, I believe, but I'm only seeing it from behind. I sniff the air. It still smells of every imaginable odor from behind me in the bazaar, but this room doesn't smell like people. Instead, it smells like brimstone and something I can't quite place. Something earthy but otherworldly. I'm guessing a demon and a fairy.

I could close the door behind me and cross to them before they'd react, but I don't know how to kill a demon. My machete is steel, so it might work for the fairy, but I suspect the oni's skin is far too hard, especially after the damage the machete took in the fight earlier. The blade would probably shatter the second it met his neck, and then I'd have three monsters ready to kill me without a way out and a whole mall-full if I somehow got past them.

I take a seat, setting my hat on the chair next to me as I smile at them. I don't think it makes it to my eyes, as I can't stop sizing them up for a fight. "Room for one more?"

The oni stares for a moment before nodding. He's a massive creature. His horns must hit the ceiling when he stands up straight.

Fighting him is seeming like an increasingly poor choice. "Buy-in is a hundred."

Shit. "I only have fifty."

"Then I guess we don't have room for one more," the fairy says. I have a better look at her now. She's tall, almost as tall as the oni, and her features are gaunt, but strangely, it doesn't make her look skeletal or alien like it would on anyone else, only more beautiful.

"Now, now," the demon says, winking at me. He looks disgustingly human but far too perfect, like a trap set to trick his prey. I thought I saw a tail when I walked in, but he seems to only have the normal human limbs now, with dark hair and dark eyes. "I'm sure there's some arrangement we can come to. Haven't you got anything else to bet?"

Normally, I only take a safe bet. I can smell when people are bluffing, and if need be, I can run faster than they can see. I won't have those advantages today, but without the money, I doubt I'll find the bastard, and then what's the point? I grab my keys and the cash I have. "I have a truck. Surely that and the cash is enough to buy in."

"What kind?" the oni asks.

I could lie, but the make is on the keys. "A Toyota, it's an older one."

"Count it as five hundred," the demon says. "I think she's good for it."

The oni shrugs and takes the money and keys before doling out five hundred and fifty dollars in chips to me. The truck has to be worth more than that, but if I can win, then I suppose it won't matter. Though it'll suck if I have to go all in and don't get the full value of my vehicle. I suppose beggars can't be choosers.

"Thank you."

The demon grins. He seems affable enough, even friendly. It makes it that much harder not to take his head. I doubt it'd actually kill him. He holds out his hand. "I'm James."

Great. A friendly game, I suppose. I choke back the bile as I take his hand and smile back, hating that I know my fangs must be visible. "Kalila."

"A pleasure." There's a button on the table, so that means it's likely Texas Hold'em. It doesn't actually say dealer on it or anything so useful, but I can make assumptions. "This big lug is Henry, and the beautiful woman to my left is Louise."

I shake the massive three-fingered hand of the oni, but Louise doesn't offer hers. "Odd name for an oni."

He grunts, and his gnarled teeth show in what I believe may be a smile, but it looks far too menacing. "I don't see why. I'm from Connecticut." I suppose the fact that he doesn't sound Japanese should've clued me in there. I've never heard of an oni in the States, though, so it is strange.

"That makes perfect sense. I apologize," I say. It hurts to do it. I hate to apologize to a man-eating monster when I should be killing it, but I know how annoying it is for people to make those sorts of assumptions. "What's the blind?"

"Ten for the big blind," the oni says. "Five for small."

I put a five in front of me, and James puts his ten. The oni deals two cards apiece, and they go around calling until it gets back to me. I have a five and a queen, spades and diamonds respectively. I call, tossing in another five, and the oni deals out the flop, setting three cards on the center of the table.

A six, a seven, and a queen. I keep myself from smiling. It's far from a win, but it's enough that I'm willing to raise my bet when it gets to me. James adds a hundred to the pot. It's possible he has two queens, but it's unlikely when I already have the one, depending on how many decks this is, so it's more likely he's going for a straight. If he has a four and an eight, then that could be a risky, if good, move. I add another hundred. Why would I ever want to be careful with my money? I'll figure out how to kill a demon if he takes everything.

He calls, and the other two fold. Shit. That's not a good sign. I eye the demon. He looks as smug and full of himself as you'd expect for that sort, but I don't have enough experience to say that it's normal. I've mostly dealt with vampires, ghouls, and a few fairies that were causing too much trouble. I've only met one demon before, and I ran like, well, hell.

Normally, I'd sniff the air to see if he was bluffing. Once you get used to picking up on the various endorphins that humans produce, it's a lot surer of a method than watching for a tell, but all I get is faint brimstone. Maybe he's not possessing a body but simply making one, so he doesn't bother with more human odors if he doesn't want them.

Henry stinks of a few scents I'd rather not place, including rotten human flesh that has to be churning away in his stomach, but he's not playing. The fairy only smells of flowers and earth. I'm going to have to actually play fair for once. I don't like it. Even as fast I am, I doubt I can cheat under these bastards' eyes. Henry deals the turn. The queen of hearts.

I eye James, letting the slightest bit of fear creep in around my eyes. If he's half as observant as I try to be, then any more than that will look like I'm faking. So long as we're using a single deck, I've all but won. There's no way he has more than one queen, so unless the next card finishes his straight, the best he can have is three pair with a slightly higher extra card. It could still win, but it's so unlikely that there's no reason to assume it.

Going all in will likely scare him off, so I raise by two hundred.

He looks me up and down, and I tap a finger on my cards while giving a fragile facade of confidence. It's a pretty standard expression for a bluff that I've seen on dozens of players.

"I fold." He tosses his hand in.

What? I barely keep from saying it out loud. I modeled it perfectly. He clearly has experience playing if he's one of the only people in the casino, so he should've thought I was bluffing.

He smirks. "I thought so."

Goddamn it. Demons are better observers than I thought. I must've let my shock show for an instant.

I take the meager hundred and twenty in winnings, and the dealing chip and deck are slid over to me. It's definitely a single deck. Fifty-two cards.

"What did you think?" Henry asks.

"She's a very good bluffer," he says. "I was playing poker back when it was first invented. I can read every tell. If you want to win against me, it's gonna come down to luck."

I grind my teeth. "Who says I was bluffing?"

He chuckles and tosses in the five for his blind.

I shuffle and deal, trying not to think about how over my head I'm in. I already made money. The extra hundred isn't much, but I could probably use it to buy the information I need and maybe still have some left to find a human poker game and win enough to get by. Anyone with a brain would do it.

But that would mean letting monsters win.

I've already let two monsters beat me. I'm not keen on letting it reach five. Or three. Henry and Louise aren't real competition. He is, the monster who thinks he's so much better than me and that he can see through everything I do. The last demon I met scared me half as much as this one does, but I'm no stranger to monsters now, and I'm not going to run again.

The next hand, I watch him closely, trying to find any sort of tell, but I end up with nothing and fold when Louise raises by a hundred on the turn. He calls her, and she wins with two pairs to his one, but he doesn't seem surprised or even annoyed. He smiles as she takes the chips. Does he not care if he wins or loses? Would've been great if he'd shown that when I had three queens.

I need to test that. I'll take enough from him to make him care.

It's his turn to deal, and he shuffles dramatically, the cards flying through the air and piling perfectly as he flicks them into place and neatly deals them to sit precisely in front of us, the bottom edges overlapping exactly the same on each pair of cards.

An eight and a four. Technically, it could get me a straight, but it's not a safe bet. They're both clubs, so I could hope for a flush. I match the blind and wait for the flop. A seven, a jack, and a six.

Two hearts and a spade. I'm not getting that flush, but I could still end up with that straight. I raise by fifty.

He raises by two hundred. The other two fold.

I stare at my chips. This is a stupid risk. I never do this. I don't gamble. I use my abilities to make sure I always have enough money to survive. It's fair payment for spending my life hunting monsters and keeping people safe. The lie rings hollow even in my own head, but it's the best justification I have, as if I actually care about keeping people safe and not simply slaughtering these monsters. "I raise." I put in another hundred.

He calls.

He must actually have something.

Shit.

The turn is a four. I have a pair at least. Barely.

He checks.

I do the same.

He's watching me. I can feel those cold demonic eyes on me. They're an iridescent red, looking more like those in a red-light district than the hellfire one would expect. But they're just as evil. If he takes everything, I'll wait for him to leave and take his head. I don't need to start a fight with an oni or a fairy.

The river is another seven. I can win with two pair. I'll be okay.

I raise by another hundred.

He raises by one hundred and twenty.

That's all I have.

He's trying to bankrupt me.

But he doesn't know I actually have anything. I didn't get my straight, but it's still a winning hand. I'll be okay. I can't fold this late in the hand. That hundred and twenty would barely get me anything. I call.

He has three sevens.

I've lost.

With a massive grin, he pulls the pile to him. "Oh, don't tell me you're out of the game already."

"You know I am," I growl. I barely keep from calling him a bastard.

"Well, then, let's fix that, why don't we? Surely you have something else to bet." He looks me over again.

I start to stand. I should storm out. But he has my truck. It doesn't matter. I have a plan. I'll kill him.

"Hmm. What was that jingling?" he asks.

I stare at him. What is he...oh. I touch the gold necklace around my throat. We didn't have a proper wedding, but we still had these at least. "I'm not selling it."

"Well, you won't get far without your vehicle."

My hand tightens into a fist, but I shove it in my pocket. My machete is practically burning against my back. I can take his head before any of them react. But will it kill him? Demons make things so complicated. "I'm sure there's something else I can pawn. This jacket cost a couple hundred." It didn't.

"Sure, maybe you could get fifty bucks here or a hundred if you can find someone dumb enough at one of the stands. But you'd lose it right after. It's not enough to try to win everything back. Or you could bet that shiny gold necklace."

I grip it. I never take it off. It's all I have left of her. We had to say our vows in secret or risk going to prison. Or worse. Her face flashes in my mind, a smile that her cheeks could barely contain as she clipped the necklace behind my neck, her lips pressing against mine.

Her lying motionless and broken on the ground next to our bed, barely even a trickle of blood around her after that bastard drained her. Our son next to her with a look of confusion and shock permanently etched on his face, burnt in my mind forever.

All that matters is killing him.

I take it off, feeling naked and wrong at the loss. "It's solid gold."

He nods. "Henry, give her two thousand in chips. Let's see if she can win this all back." He grins, watching as I set the necklace on the table, forcing myself not to cry. "God, it's better than sex."

I can see his head rolling on the table so vividly that for a second, I think I actually did it, but my machete is still in its sheath, and his head is still on his shoulders. The demon grins, his eyes seeming to invite me to dance with him down to hell. Of course, judging by the expression on his face, that dance may be euphemistic. My stomach turns. I'd sooner burn.

Louise deals the cards. A king and a queen. I can work with this.

I check. He raises. As ever. Why does he play at such a low stakes table if he always makes it cost a few hundred? Though I suppose I shouldn't complain when I need to take a few thousand.

I call. I'm not getting cocky yet.

The flop is a queen, a king, and a seven. I have two pair. I've won thousands with just that before, but the last time I was so sure of myself, I lost my truck.

Then again, I can't let those doubts get to me. They'll make me stupid. I can't cheat, but I can at least keep my head. Longer than he will.

He raises again.

I do the same.

His perfect teeth show in a broad smile, strangely sinister in how friendly it is. "You don't want to lose everything again, do you, Kalila?"

"Doesn't seem likely, why, are you getting worried you will?" I ask.

He chuckles, and it's oddly disconcerting. It's perfect, friendly, warm, happy, and every positive feeling one could associate with a laugh, and all coming from the mouth of a manipulative, sadistic demon who's trying to take the only thing I have left of Lakia. "I like you. You should come to these games more often. Why haven't I seen you before?"

"I'm not from Toronto."

"I can hear that." He laughs again, and it's exactly as perfect. "What brought you to Toronto? Business or pleasure?"

Great. Lying isn't going to get me anywhere. "Revenge." Maybe I just want to see his response. Not that I'd be so lucky as to scare him, but it might distract him from the game.

He sits up, the smile growing wider, changing the shape of his face as he covers his cards on the table. "Now that is a compelling answer. What are you getting revenge for?"

"Why does anyone get revenge?"

He shrugs and tosses in the chips to call me. "There are so many reasons. Some quite compelling and some dreadfully dull. Tell me, Kalila, what are yours?"

Why do I want to tell him? Is this some demonic power, or is it simply nice to not have to lie? "He killed my family and moved here. I'm going to kill him, but I need to find him first. I've heard this is the best place to get information."

"That it is. The Community Center is the best place to get nearly anything."

The other two must've folded without my noticing, as they don't even have cards. Louise tosses out the turn, a ten.

Shit. If he's going for a straight, he may have it now. I raise but only by a hundred. I need to test him. If he thinks I have a straight, he won't bet, but if he has one…

He raises.

He's bluffing.

He has to be.

I have two pairs. A straight isn't impossible, but it's not likely yet.

But he could have it.

I'll lose everything if I'm stupid enough to call the bet.

I raise again.

Laughing, he calls me.

The river is a king.

I have a full house with three kings. That's a hell of a winning hand.

But he could have a straight.

"Who is this guy you're looking for?" he asks. "He have a name?"

He's trying to get in my head. That has to be a good sign. I raise. "His name's Gregory Reynolds." I take the picture from my pocket and hold it out to him. "The blond guy."

"With the open shirt? Very sexy, for a murderer. Though I suppose I could say the same of you."

"What was that?" My hand slips behind my back without my meaning to. He dares compare me to that monster?

"Hmm." He raises by another hundred and smiles. "He looks familiar."

"Where have you seen him?"

He stares at the picture, not taking his eyes off it. Finally, he looks up at me, beaming. "I'm not certain. Maybe he was in an ad. I couldn't say."

God, but I want to wipe that smile from his face. "I'm all in."

The smile only grows, his face contorting more, growing rounder. "Oh, Kalila. You are so fun. I'm afraid you have more chips than I do."

I stare at the pile in front of him and at my own bet. "I suppose I do."

"Then perhaps I can sweeten the pot. I do so hate the idea that I couldn't clean you out if I win. If you're left with something, it's hardly gambling, is it? You understand, don't you?"

"What did you have in mind?"

"In truth, while he does look familiar, I don't know him." He slides the picture back to me, and I snatch it from the table, nearly flipping my cards. "But I know who you could talk to in order to find out. Both of the best options, in fact. I'll even introduce you."

I'm not sure I'm willing to spend any more time around him than absolutely necessary. But revenge is always necessary. "If you can live up to that."

"I can," he purrs.

My skin crawls. "I'll take it. Give him the chips."

"I'm not sure how to..." Henry shrugs "Okay." He gives James enough to match me, and he goes all in.

A full house. He has two queens and the one from the table, with the two kings. It's an amazing hand. It'd be sure to beat anyone.

But my full house is better.

His smile only grows. "Oh, that was nail-biting." He chuckles. "Give her back her stuff and the winnings. I haven't had that much fun in months."

I glower at him.

"Such a pretty smile." He keeps laughing. It should be annoying by now, but it's so melodic. "How about we go meet my favorite information broker?"

CHAPTER EIGHT

James grins as we walk out of the casino. My necklace is safely restored to its rightful place, and my hat is back on my head. "Since you're new here, why don't I give you the proper tour?"

I glower at him. He's been nothing but annoying since I met him, and I have only grown to like him less. "Or you could take me to the information broker you promised."

"The first broker is on the other side of the Community Center. It only seems neighborly to give you the tour first."

What would happen if I cut his head off? He wouldn't die, but surely, it would hurt. Would it regrow? "I don't have the time nor the inclination for a tour."

He grins, his eyes glinting. "Your wish is my command."

"Sure doesn't feel like it."

With his perfect laugh, he leads the way. "May I at least say what we're passing since I'm not allowed to go out of my way to give you a tour?"

I groan. At a certain point, it's easier to let him talk. "Fine."

"I'm sure you've seen the market. There's an excellent pastry shop run by a couple of fauns and a few weapon shops I'm sure you'd appreciate now that you have my money to spend."

"It's my money now."

"That it is. Vitaly has a particularly good stock, and he's a friend, so I may be able to get you a discount."

My machete *is* falling apart. "What would this discount cost me?"

"Not a thing. I did say I was being neighborly, didn't I? I enjoyed our game. I'd like to play more."

I grunt. "I enjoyed winning your money. I enjoyed it a lot less when you insisted I gamble with my necklace."

"I knew you'd win."

I cross my arms to keep from grabbing my weapon. "I'm sure you did."

"I can read the cards."

"Right."

He chuckles. It's oddly dryer but equally musical. "Fine, don't believe me." He gestures to the side. "That's a meeting room where a bunch of support groups are held. I'm in the one for not eating humans. I'm sure they have something that could help with your bloodlust."

"I'm not—"

"The revenge, not the vampirism."

"Shut up and take me to the broker."

He turns and traces a finger along his lip in a way that seems unnervingly lewd, pockets an imaginary key, and takes me farther down the hall, past all of the stands with sundry goods. "This is it," he finally says, pointing to an opening in the wall where a shutter must've once been but has long since been removed. "I trust talking in this instance is acceptable?"

"Who is he?"

"His name is Vincent. I'll manage the introduction, as he doesn't tend to like working with strangers, but he should hopefully have what you're looking for. The other broker isn't here too often." He leads me inside, and I'm shocked to find it's a fairly orderly store. I expected an information broker in a shutterless dive in an abandoned mall to be hiding out in storage or have a wreck of a storefront, but it's a fairly organized tobacco shop. It almost smells like my father.

I don't recognize the creature behind the counter. It's humanoid, though discolored in a way that's hard to describe. It doesn't look dead or sickly or any unnatural color, it simply doesn't look like the skin of a human. "James," he says. Whatever Vincent is, he sounds like a soft spoken, effete Irish guy. That has to mean he's another fairy. I'd never seen so many fairies in my life, but of course, they'd all be here. It gives them more people to screw over. "Who's your friend?"

"An old poker buddy," James replies, leaning against the counter. I resist glaring at him over the accusation that I'm his buddy or have known him longer than the miserable hour I've already had to spend with him. It's simply dishonest. "She was hoping to ask you a question. I'd appreciate it if you'd help her as a favor for me."

His eyes light up. Literally. "A favor? You so rarely cash those in, James. What makes this poker buddy so special?"

"That's between me and him," I say.

"Hmm." Vincent looks me up and down, his not-quite-human eyes seeming to study my very soul. I wonder if I still have one. He gives an appreciative nod. I suppose that means I do. My heart sinks. I preferred the idea that I am animated by vengeance; it means my soul can be with my wife, where it belongs. My still having my soul would mean that anything I do here could further damn me. But I'm only killing monsters. I'll still make it to her. She'll just have to wait until I finish killing all of them or die trying. "Very well, what is your question?"

With the way he speaks about favors, it sounds like he's a particularly old-fashioned fairy, and that only makes him more dangerous. Theoretically, he may not be able to lie, but I can't be certain. I haven't met enough of them to know how they work. I only have what I've read and my experience with the one I gambled with. "I'm looking for this man." I slide the picture over, indicating Reynolds. "Do you know anything about him?"

He purses his lips, staring at it. "I have never seen any of the people in this picture before. May I have his name?"

I've heard so many times that you shouldn't give a fairy a name when they ask for it, but I'd love for him to do the worst he can with Reynolds's name. "Gregory Reynolds. He was a private in the American military, and now he's hiding in Toronto. He's a vampire. That's what I know. Do you recognize any of that?"

"I have to look over my files." He looks at the picture again and shakes his head. He spins, knocking over a cup of pencils on his desk while he rummages through a drawer. I right it and put the seven pencils back where they go. "Ah, Gregory Reynolds. He came here about eighteen years ago. Why are you looking for him now?"

"I gave you plenty. What more can you tell me?"

He sighs. "I'm afraid that I can't honor my favor, James. You know how much that pains me. There's nothing I can tell you that you don't already know. He's a vampire in Toronto, and he ran here after he was called back to Iraq."

I do my best to keep from showing any reaction. If he thinks he told me anything new, he might expect payment. Granted, if James is the one who'd owe it, I'm happy to have him pay, but I don't know that he won't charge me as well. I never knew why Reynolds came to Canada. Perhaps he avoided Iraq since he was scared he'd meet me again. It hurts to keep from smirking at that thought. "You don't know anything else?"

"There's nothing more I can say. I'm sorry."

"But there is something more you know?"

His teeth show, but I'd hesitate to call it a smile. They're slightly sharper than human teeth but in a way that seems to depend on the angle. "I've never met the man. I've said all that I can tell you. But I know many things."

"About him."

The teeth seem to grow sharper. "Would you like me to tell you how many teeth he has? There's nothing useful I can say. I've never met him, I've had no communication with him, and I don't know where you can find him. Nor do I know his weaknesses, beyond that I suspect taking off his head would kill him. So unless you want to keep accusing me of not adequately answering your question, when I already told you that I don't know, I'd appreciate it if you left."

I feel like he knows something more, but I suspect one always feels that way around the fae, and that they quite like it that way.

I stride out of the shop and turn to James. "Well, that was a waste of time. Where's the other one?"

"She doesn't tend to be at the Community Center. She also doesn't like me."

"Can't imagine why."

He smirks, and there's something in it that's so disconcerting I take a step back. I don't like demons. "I can give you her address. Will that suffice? I'd hate to still be in your debt."

The idea of him owing me anything bothers me almost as much as my owing him would. Being around him makes my skin crawl. "Sure, that works."

He pats his pockets and smiles. "I don't suppose you have a pen and paper?"

I don't want to give this creep my phone. "You can tell me the address, and I'll put it in."

Still grinning, he recites it, and I type it into my phone and screenshot it to make sure Maps doesn't lose it.

"How about we finish your tour?"

"I'm good."

"I did say I'd show you where to buy weapons, didn't I?"

My machete presses against my back, and I know it will break in the next fight or the one after. I can probably find it myself, but I don't want to have to spend any more time talking to these monsters than I absolutely have to. "All right. Fine. Show me before I regret it."

He grabs my hand and drags me on. I manage to yank it free to that same laugh as he guides me through stand after stand, saying bits of random information, like what wretched monster runs them or how amazing some item from them is. I barely listen. I want him to shut up. I wouldn't even be going along with him if my machete wasn't falling apart.

Finally, we arrive at a stand with swords, axes, knives, and a few guns. There are price tags on them, and they're surprisingly reasonable. I suppose there is an upside to coming to monstrous black markets: there are no background checks. I had to leave my old pistol in Ohio since I didn't want more trouble crossing the border; I already look eighteen years younger than the age on my passport, in addition to the general pleasures of traveling as a Middle Eastern woman.

The creature behind the counter looks almost human. His features are far too perfect, and his skin is only barely off-color, but I don't think he's a fairy. He doesn't smell as earthy or preternatural as they tend to. He smells dead. Not like rot or decay but simply like the absence of life, like how a rock or piece of metal smells dead.

"How may I help you, young lady?" he asks. His accent is Slavic but faint.

Compared to him, I probably am young. Most immortals live to be quite old, until they meet me. I hate that I have to let him keep living, but I'm not sure what it'd take to kill him. He's not a vampire, and other undead can be unpredictable. "Just looking for some weapons."

"And what are you hunting?"

I glare at him.

"Well, if you're planning on hunting me, I think you'll struggle. I'd advise you not to test anything here. It tends to hurt."

"Isn't that the idea?"

"You."

I stare. What creatures reflect harm? That's strange. "I'm hunting vampires."

"Are vampires ever not trying to kill each other?"

I take a deep breath. If I try to kill him, it sounds like it'll kill me instead. I can't die until I kill Reynolds. I'll never be able to tolerate being called a vampire. I pick up a machete from the table. It feels sturdy. Mine was a cheap, mass-produced one, while this is heavy and made of a single piece of steel with a wrap on one end. The balance heavily favors the tip, making it perfect for beheading. "What guns do you have?"

"That would work on vampires? Crossbows, if stakes work on them."

"Bullets still hurt."

"Can't imagine." He chuckles and gestures toward a meager selection of pistols and long guns. "It's not my main area, but I've been trying to branch out. I have a few classic flintlocks as well."

"I'll stick with something made in the last century." I pick up a revolver. It's massive for my hands, and they're not tiny. "A .44?"

He nods.

I pop the release to see six slots in the cylinder. I was hoping for eight, but at least with a .44, I'll have the stopping power for anything. The six hundred dollars on the price tag will eat into a good portion of my winnings, but I can always get more, and I need to be alive more than I need money. "This gun, the machete, and a few boxes of bullets."

"That'll be seven hundred."

It should be almost eight, but maybe he's rounding down. I do like nice round numbers. I hand over the money, mutter thank you to the monster, and head for the door. I should still have a holster in my suitcase that will fit this.

"You don't want the rest of the tour?" James asks, following me.

"Why are you so insistent? I agreed to the weapons, but now I have someplace to go."

"Well, the auction is about to start, and I thought you might want to see it."

My blood would run cold if there was enough pumping through my veins. "What auction?"

His smile turns more wicked. "The human one. Where we sell various hunters that were captured trying to break in here or victims that other fiends caught while hunting."

"What?" It's all I can manage to say. I've spent this whole time trying to pretend I wasn't surrounded by the worst scum in the entire world, save for Reynolds, and there was a slave market going on under my nose? I should've killed them all when I first got here.

"As a hunter, I thought you might find it interesting. You might have some comrades up for sale."

My mouth goes dry. "Where?"

"I thought you didn't want the tour?"

I grab him by his collar, but he only smirks more. "Where the fuck is the auction?"

His grin grows past his cheeks, and he gestures behind us to the back of the mall, but I didn't need to ask. Now that I'm looking, I can hear it, smell it. There are so many scents, and human fills this place. There's one in the other corner, those pies there are full of it, but there's so much more coming from where he's pointing. Alive and scared. And I can hear the cry of an auctioneer.

I drop the demonic bastard and start moving farther into the mall. I just came from there. How did I miss it? Am I so obsessed that I missed...no, I didn't miss it. I can smell humans everywhere. I let myself ignore people suffering because I needed money and information.

I load the gun and put it in the back of my pants, then stuff the boxes of bullets in my jacket pockets. They don't fit well, but I need to get rid of the bag if I'm going to fight. I pick up speed, holding one machete already and drawing my other one.

These bastards won't get away with this.

The auction hall is cramped. Dozens of monsters of all shapes and sizes fill it, while on a wooden stage in the back are two more fiends with five humans.

I recognize one of them.

It doesn't make sense. It's not possible. Why would that kid be here? The leader of his little gang warned me off coming here. Why would he be here on his own? None of the other people are from his crew.

His eyes find me. He's gagged, but the contempt in them is unmistakable. He sees me as another monster. It's all he ever saw me as.

I convinced everyone else, but he never bought it. Then why did he come here? Did he think he'd catch me in the act? Did I get this kid captured?

I can see my own son sitting in his place. I blink, willing the image away. I was going to kill these bastards anyway. Now I have a better reason to.

I rush the stage.

The monsters don't have time to react. I shove through the crowd. I should kill them all. I'm not entirely sure why I don't. They're literally buying slaves. But my eyes are locked on the auctioneer, and the second my feet touch the stage, his head joins them. The new machete cleaves through him like a dream. I stare at it, resisting the urge to lick the blood off. It's a vile practice that I've never given into on more than a handful of occasions.

A cry echoes around me. I'm not sure if it's shock or rage, but I turn to the crowd. For a second, I think I'll be able to give them a speech on why I did what I did and that maybe they'll be cowed into the orderly conduct I've seen at the rest of this bazaar, but instead, they start climbing onto the stage.

"Shit," I mutter. They're fast, but I'm faster than most, and I'm closer. I hurry to the nearest captive and cut him free. It's not the kid, but it's a start. He rubs his wrists, blinking in confusion and looking around.

I swing for the restraints on the next one, and I think I hit them, but something tackles me to the back wall, a clawed hand tightening around my throat.

I gasp for air and fail, but that reminds me that I don't actually need oxygen, that I breathe more out of habit than anything else. I slice off the hand, but more grab me and pin me to the wall. They press in hard enough that I scream and drop my machetes, hearing an unpleasant crack from one of my wrists and the cheap machete as it hits the ground.

Masses of monsters press against me. Some are drooling. They want to eat me. To make me pay. I hear voices muttering, but I can't understand them over the pain in my hand. It's broken. Again. I just fixed that arm.

I blink, trying to make sense of the world. I don't recognize the tentacled thing pinning my legs, nor the creature that broke my wrist, though I know it's the one I chopped the hand off of, but at least I can identify that there's a vampire baring its fangs at me. I knew I should've studied up on more monsters if I was going into this business, but it never seemed to come up. Now I'm going to die, again, before I get my revenge, and I won't even know what killed me.

"Oh God, you've made quite a mess," a familiar voice says from the back of the crowd. I can't place it at first. They're still pressing on my broken wrist, pinning me by it. My other is near the point of snapping as well. This creature is so heavy and so strong.

It has a long snout and a furry face, and its hot breath keeps pelting my face with saliva as it presses down. I meet its beady eyes, glaring into them, and it presses down harder with its only hand, crushing the bones to dust. With nothing left to prop it up, my hand sickeningly slackens against the creature's fingers. "Back off, demon," it bellows, the words spraying me with spittle. At first, I think it means me, and I'd happily do so if I was able.

But the other voice clicks into place. "I'm afraid my payment to this idiot still isn't complete."

It bares its teeth but doesn't turn from me. They're wretched, miscolored, jagged things. "Did you see what she did? Her life is forfeit. She killed another fiend in the Community Center. And cut off the hand of another." It holds up its own hand for emphasis. Its words are like a monstrous growl shaped into English. It's disconcerting that it's so intelligible.

I try to form a response. I'm not sure if I'll apologize, make my case, or insult it, but I can't make words. My larynx seems to be crumbling under the grasp of one of these monsters. The world flashes, and I try to keep my eyes open only to find that I haven't actually closed them. I simply can't see through the pain.

James's voice comes through the fog. "Well, you seem to be doing a good job paying that pain back. And the wound did seem to be inflicted in self-defense."

"The killing wasn't," it growls.

"Yes, so we'll kick her out. That is the rule, is it not? It's not like for like. Need I remind you that you're violating the rules yourself right now? All of you are. You're inflicting harm upon another fiend here."

The pressure relaxes the barest bit, and the vague forms of creatures appear through the blinding darkness and look between themselves.

"I've never actually seen a fight here before," one mutters.

"How do they normally handle it?"

"They normally don't," James says. "It's not typically an issue. Unfortunately, some people are too stupid to abide by the rules."

I attempt a pithy response, but words still aren't working.

"So we kick them out. She's banned from here now. No one who's harmed another fiend on Community Center grounds is allowed back. Perhaps you might want to all turn around and walk away because otherwise, you all know exactly who else has harmed a fiend on these grounds."

"Well, she's already being kicked out," one says.

"She hasn't had the chance to leave yet. In fact, you're holding her here. Hardly seems sporting."

The furry creature growls but pulls its hand away. My own hand presses against my wrist in a way that I'm glad I can't see.

"Are you certain we're not supposed to kill them?"

James steps up. The monsters must've made room. His too-perfect face comes into focus. "I'm quite certain."

It growls. "She took my hand."

"Go see Dr. Sun. I'm sure she can fix you right up." He kneels and comes back up holding the still-bleeding furry mitt of the creature. "Best hurry, though."

It snaps its teeth right in front of my face and snatches its hand, stomping away.

"You're an idiot," James says.

I open my mouth, and a choking sound comes out.

"You better hope that Dorenia can help you because you killed every other lead you could've had."

I look toward the captives. The one I cut free is still sitting there. The kid is still glaring at me. He's not trying to speak, though. He's not saying anything through his gag.

"They're not letting you leave with them. They're property. And they don't want to go anywhere."

I try to say, "The kid," but only a hoarse croak comes out.

He shakes his head. "I don't owe you that much."

I pull myself to my feet. I can barely stand. They didn't break my ankles, but they got close. There's no way I can run with him. I look around. It's a market. An auction. Maybe I can buy his freedom. I fish in my pocket for my wallet, my numb hand struggling to pull it out.

"No. The auction will be delayed. And you can't buy here anymore."

I grit my teeth, glaring at him, but his face stays placid.

"I'm taking you out of here. If I don't do so within the next minute, I suspect you'll be right back in the situation from which I've just rescued you. Don't waste the life I saved."

I gasp, trying to choke out a "fuck you," but he only laughs that melodious laugh. I pick up my unbroken machete along with my trampled hat. I want to take his head.

But he's the only thing keeping me alive right now.

I cut the kid free and shove him.

"What the hell are you doing?" James asks.

The kid slumps. I shove him again.

"They keep them in a stupor. A siren, I believe."

I don't hear any singing. I should only have to break him out of it. I struggle to snap my fingers before his eyes, and he blinks.

I shove him again, and he topples onto his side. Goddamn it. Get up, kid. Run.

James grabs my hand, and I buckle to my knees in pain.

"Ah, that's broken." He grips the other and drags me with a strength I can barely imagine. I don't even end up on my feet. I'm simply on the stage one second and at the door the next. "Get out and never come back. I believe this covers my debt."

I open my mouth.

"Stop trying to cuss me out and get out of here."

I stare past him. I can no longer see the stage, but the kid still has to be there. I mouth, "Please." I'm desperate enough that I'm asking a demon for help.

He grimaces. "My next poker game is at my house. You'll be there."

If that's what it takes. I nod.

"I'll buy the child's freedom, but you will owe me quite greatly for this, and I promise, I will collect."

I stumble out of the mall on half-functioning legs and barely make it to my truck before I collapse. I drive back to my hotel one-handed and try not to think about what it might mean to be in a demon's debt.

CHAPTER NINE

K nocking at the door wakes me from the fire. I rub my eyes as best I can with one hand, trying to shake the same images I always wake up with. It's the only time I ever see my family, and yet I so desperately wish not to. I struggle to my feet. My ankles are still weak, but I manage to drag myself to the door and hand over the cash for the blood delivery. Toronto does have its conveniences. I slam the door in the monster's face and collapse onto the bed, draining the entire bag until my hand doesn't dangle uselessly and my bones are solid.

"Fuck," I mutter, finding my throat no longer sore or crushed.

I stare at the bag, my stomach turning over in revulsion. I keep giving in. I'm better than this. I'm not another monster. All I can see are those poor people being sold like cattle. How am I any better when I'm feeding from them too? Taking donor blood from the humans who actually need it.

I glare at the ceiling. It's a tacky tile design. I don't have time to hate myself.

Once I've washed the blood from my lips, I grab a clean bra, shirt, and holster from my suitcase, throw on my jeans, jacket, and hat, and head out to meet the only lead I have left.

Did I make a bad decision?

If this dealer can't tell me anything, I don't have shit. I'm banned from the Community Center, but how could I live with myself if I hadn't done everything in my power to save humans who are being victimized? It's the only thing I have left keeping *me* human.

I grip my necklace, the only other link to my old life. I left my home, my friends, and my family. I've given myself completely to revenge. But I'll never give myself to being a monster.

I made the right decision. It might cost me, but there was no other option.

The broker's address is in Toronto proper, far from my cheap hotel, but I have enough cash that I don't need to worry about running out of gas, and hopefully, I'll still be able to afford whatever information she has.

Her name's Dorenia Shaw. That's all I know. I don't even know what sort of creature to expect.

I pull up in front of a warehouse across from a Tim Horton's. It's not abandoned like I'd expected. It looks actively in use. Maybe she runs an import-export business? It's the sort of shady business these kinds of assholes run. A sign on the side seems to confirm that, but it's faded enough that it could belong to the previous owner. If that is her business, attracting customers clearly isn't the focus. It might be a way to launder money, which would suggest she has a legal identity, so she was once human and maybe not centuries old. Though if a person has enough money, I'm sure they can have an identity made that would stand up to any government scrutiny so long as they paid their taxes.

I need to look into that soon. The way that border agent looked at me over my passport means I can't use it anymore. The excuse that I look good for fifty-two won't hold up for much longer.

The door by the parking lot is locked. I knew I should've called first, but I don't like letting people know I'm coming. They tend to want to kill me. I go around the back, looking for another entrance. The loading bay doors are wide open, and vans are parked outside them. Something about it makes the hair on the back of my neck stand on end. This doesn't look like a delivery. They're parked with the fronts facing the building rather than the backs for them to actually carry whatever they're moving, but I also don't hear the sounds of people moving freight. It's too quiet. I close my eyes, listening. Footsteps thud in the warehouse. They don't smell human.

Vampires? The scent of blood lingers on them, but it's not fresh. It's definitely vampires. I reach for my machete but hesitate. What am I walking into? Are they hunting for this information broker? Who is she? What could she have done?

My machete is already in my left hand and my revolver in my right. Apparently, I don't care about those answers as much as I thought I did. They're vampires who broke in and are hunting someone, and I'm a vampire hunter. Finding out why they're here can wait.

I open my eyes and stride inside, not bothering to worry about the reasons or the participants. I can find out what the hell's going on when they're all dead.

I sniff the air. They're not close. Their footsteps echo through the large warehouse, but it's too full for me to see them. Boxes and crates are everywhere, with only a few open enough to take a look at the contents. The one near me has rugs. It's possible there's something underneath, but I don't care enough to investigate.

There are vampires to kill.

My footsteps are nearly silent, but if they're not too focused on their prey, they'll still hear me. There's no sense in hiding. At least five of them. No, six, but the other is farther off. If I had any sense, I'd take them out one at a time. I used to do it like that, systematic, careful, but they're all together, and I want my prey. I've had to let too many monsters live.

I pick up speed, weaving between a few boxes, following their scent.

One of them lets out a grunt of surprise. He must have heard me. He mutters to his companions.

They sound so close. I can almost touch them. I shove a crate aside and grin as I find the five of them clustered together, kukri in their hands. It's a good weapon for beheading. Are they hunting a vampire too? Is that the sixth scent?

I should talk to them. Find out what's going on. But they're hunting my only lead. She's a vampire, then. I'm going to rescue a fucking leech, but that means, if I kill them, I might get the information I'm after.

And I would have done it for free.

They seem confused and look between each other. They're all men and bigger than me. They were moving in formation, so they're probably trained. Former military? "Is she backup?" one of them asks.

I put a bullet between his eyes.

It won't kill a vampire, not unless I shoot its head clean off, but they need their brains. Judging by the pink goo on his companions, this one is missing most of his. With enough blood, he can recover, but he won't have the wherewithal to drink on his own and will waste away to nothing, unable to die until the rest of the brain finally rots or is severed from the body. I like this gun.

Saying that they hesitate for a moment is misleading. Vampires are fast. Their reactions can barely be measured. They see something and can snatch and eat in that very instant. But for that barest nanosecond, they hold back, looking between the body on the ground and me.

It doesn't give me long enough to even raise my gun, but it tells me they're scared. They recover with speed that I'd call admirable if they weren't monsters, and rush me. I leap back, grateful that the boxes and crates keep the walkways narrow as I fire a round into another one.

It drops.

The remaining three set on me. There's barely enough room, but they know how to fight well enough not to get in each other's way. Maybe not military, then, something private and melee-focused. Some big shot vampire's special forces? A kukri flies for my throat, and I catch it on my machete and fire at its owner, but he leaps away, the bullet shattering a nearby box and sending debris everywhere.

Another one swings, and I have to leap out of the way, his weapon clipping my shoulder. It's only a scratch, and I can still use it, but their faces contort in hunger. I ate recently, and there's now almost-fresh blood in the air.

My back bumps into a crate. "Shit." The three of them stay together, standing in place. If one goes first, it'll die, and they know it. They intend to attack me all at once. I'm not faster than them or stronger, and I'm probably not better trained. All I have is that I'm more used to fighting vampires, and I know for a fact that I can't take three at once with my back to a wall.

I fire at the middle one, and the other two lunge, one going low from the right, the other high from the left. I block the high one and fire into the asshole on my right. Its kukri slices through my leg, and it lets out a blood-curdling cry. Or maybe that's me.

The other kukri presses against my weapon, and I slip, falling to my knee, tears welling in my eyes, as there's not much left of my leg. The pain is indescribable, but I try to keep myself focused, pressing back against the remaining vampire. Its lip curls into a smile, fangs showing, as something moves to my right. That one isn't dead?

I put another bullet in it, and the movement stops.

The leech pushes on me, and I topple. It's on me, its kukri stabbing at my throat. I knock the weapon aside, but it comes right back. I try to angle my gun only for the leech to grab my wrist and pin it. The kukri comes again, and I block, but the leech keeps pressing. It has size and gravity in its favor. I try to roll and almost succeed, but it slams its knee into what's left of my leg, and I scream.

My machete slips, and the kukri drops for my throat. I try another roll, and the vampire presses in on my knee.

I'm going to die. To some no-name vampire asshole who doesn't have anything to do with Reynolds.

Fuck that. I jerk, trying to shake him off me, and the kukri barely misses my neck. He pulls back, and I drop my machete, grabbing his wrist, but I can't stop him. He's going to kill me.

Blood wells up from his throat, old and dry, oozing onto me. His head rolls to the side.

I gasp for breath, sitting up and looking around as I drop his body off me. The leeches are barely moving; the few synapses still firing are simply causing them to squirm. They're gone. But someone is standing over me. A woman I don't know wearing a red blouse and a lacy black skirt. She's holding a claymore.

"Not bad," she says. "What are you doing in my warehouse?" She sounds like a Beatle. I'd expected French Canadian or maybe Russian, to live up to the reputation of former soviets turned black market merchants.

I pant, trying to ignore the pain.

"Right." She fishes in a pocket sewn into her skirt and pulls out a bag of blood. "Answers can wait."

Twice in one day. I glare at it but snatch it before she can change her mind.

I only drink half.

I'm not an animal.

I don't have to give into my worst impulses.

I have my leg back. She must've put it where it goes or else half a pint wouldn't have been enough, and the light scratch is gone. It wasn't that bad. Not like earlier.

"That's better. You looked like shit a few minutes ago."

I glare at her. I just saved a leech's life. She stinks of it, just as surely as these corpses do.

"I'm Dorenia Shaw. You must be Kalila Yassin."

I wipe my mouth and stand, looking for my machete. I could reach it, but she has her claymore on her back, and I'm not sure I'd be faster. "How do you know that?"

"Well, you're coming to see me because I'm an information broker, so I assume that would go without saying: I have sources. You're new in town and already attracting attention, or did getting kicked out of the Community Center within a week of coming to Toronto seem like the sort of thing that wouldn't pique the interest of people whose job is literally to know things?"

"Okay, maybe it was a stupid question," I mutter, picking up my weapons and putting them away. "Do you know why I'm here too?"

She smirks. For a vampire, it's not a bad smile. There's something playful and lively in it that I don't tend to see in the undead. It almost makes me think I could grow to like her, and that makes me hate her. This is what happens when I try playing nice with vampires instead of killing them. I start seeing them as people. "I have my assumptions, but why don't you tell me? I do so hate to let anything slip for free. But come, there's no need to do business next to a pile of corpses. I'll get someone to clean that up."

She grabs her phone from another pocket and says, "Yes, I have a mess I need you to take care of," then hangs up and pockets the phone without waiting for a response. She leads me to the back of the warehouse and a set of stairs. On the second floor, she opens a door leading into a room with a carpeted floor, polished wooden furniture, a record player, a mini-bar right out in the open, and a massive desk with a leather chair behind it and two red plush chairs in front of it. Part of me wonders if they were always red, but it's more of a maroon than what blood would actually dry into.

I sit across from her. "Now will you tell me?"

That same smile answers me, her cheeks dimpling. She looks almost human. A bit lighter than me, with dark brown hair in a neat bun over small ears. "You still haven't asked."

I pull out the old photo. I'm lucky no blood got on it. "Where can I find this man?" I tap him.

She nods, taking it from me and staring at it. "I could arrange a meeting, but it'll cost you."

"I saved your life. That doesn't earn me anything?"

"Did you forget that I saved yours after? And fed you. But I have a reputation to keep, and you expect me to arrange a meeting that you intend to end in bloodshed. Saving me once is hardly enough for that."

"I—"

"Don't pretend. You want to kill him. That's as clear as day in your eyes, even if you hadn't been going on about it at a poker game. You saved my life, and I do owe you, but you doing this will cost me quite a lot. I don't have a way to simply show you to him or tell you about him. If it was that easy, I don't think you'd have been searching this long, now, would you?"

I shrug, hating to concede the point. I won't let myself look excited. She'd raise the price and I can't afford to get my hopes up. I've had too many dead ends to let myself trust that this will go anywhere.

"He's connected and has been here for quite a while. Had you made better time, perhaps this would be easier, but he's expecting you. So if you want me to ruin my name just so you can get revenge, not only do I expect you to tell me why, but I expect you to make it worth my while."

I want to be angry. Or at least annoyed. But she has a point. There's no way in the world I can meet Reynolds and not take his head the second I see him. Her name would be on that. "How much?"

"Oh, you can't afford me." She chuckles, and it's not as melodic as James's, but it has that same playfulness as her smile. "I need you to kill someone. That can be payment. Then maybe these assholes will stop coming after me."

"I'm not a hitman."

"I'm sorry, let me rephrase. I need you to kill a vampire."

I can't keep from smiling. "You should've led with that."

"Then we have a deal? You take care of my problem, and I'll introduce you to yours?" She holds out her hand.

I stare at it. I've never shaken hands with a vampire before. It feels wrong. I reach out, taking it. Her grip is firm, but her hand is surprisingly soft for dead skin. I nod. "Who do you want me to kill?"

CHAPTER TEN

Dorenia

The door slammed in my face. It was the fourth one in a row, and I barely stepped back in time to avoid having my tray knocked to the ground. One of the jars sloshed and threatened to tip over, but I pressed the tray against the wall and grabbed it before it fell, panting. I could've sworn they were getting worse. It had never been easy making these sales, but people seemed to only be growing more hostile. It was never a good sign. We'd probably need to move soon if we didn't want to be driven out of town.

I secured the strap to my shoulders, making sure the toys and drinks stayed in place as I stood. There was no way they'd take kindly to my leaning against their house.

I went a bit farther up the street, hoping that this neighborhood was just worse than usual, and found a house a few roads down with the gate to its front yard open and a cobblestone path heading right to the door. It was massive, far bigger than anyplace I'd normally try selling to. I'd gone farther than I meant; this was the wealthier part of Liverpool.

Kalila stares at me, her light brown eyes narrowing. "What on earth does any of this have to do with my question? I asked who I had to kill, not for your life story."

"I'm getting there. It's important that you hear the whole thing."

"Then get there faster."

I sigh. The story needs to be told a certain way to have the proper flair, and if it doesn't have adequate impact, I doubt I'll make it out of this business relationship alive. She may kill him first, but I'd rather avoid being killed second. Or third. "I will, I promise, we're almost there. You need to know the context to understand how important this is."

I looked at the door and back down the road. We needed the money. But what were the chances they'd want anything? They could buy far nicer from anywhere else.

Though any alcohol would be weaker. I'd focus on that. Maybe I couldn't beat the impossible quality of the goods they could order, but I could certainly beat the strength. The prices weren't labeled, so I could easily raise them to match the sort of expectations they'd have. Novelty and strength, I'd focus on that, and try to get a sale.

The path was impressively smooth and maintained and led up to a polished oak door. Taking a deep breath, I knocked.

The better part of a minute flew by without any sound coming from the other side. I was ready to give up when finally, it flew open, and a woman in a gown made of fabric that had to cost more than I'd make in a year looked out at me. "Can I help you?" she asked. It wasn't what I expected. She wasn't throwing me out, but it also wasn't the formal greeting that I'd assumed one would receive at a place like this.

"I was hoping to help you, actually." I smiled. "I have a number of goods for sale, including some rather potent alcohol from the East." Technically, the still was east of here, so it wasn't a lie.

"I..." She looked behind her. "I'm not sure the master of the house will be interested."

I tried to contain my disappointment. It was better treatment than I'd received in a while, even if it wasn't a sale.

"But we might be. Come around back to the servants' entrance and let us see what you have. We so rarely have time to go out to do our own shopping."

A smile pulled at my cheeks. That was the best news I'd had in days. "I'll be right there."

The servants' entrance was in a recess at the back of the house, but it was easy enough to find, and the door was open and waiting for me. They marveled at my selection, poring over everything. A few kids jumped at the chance to have some proper toys, grabbing a doll and a carved horse and carriage while the men grabbed bottle after bottle of alcohol. The cloths I had didn't seem to interest the women, but one begged for me to read her palm. I'd never learned the trade, but I'd seen it done enough times that I wasn't willing to say no.

She sat by the counter, and one of the men pushed a chair over for me, so I sat and took her hand. I muttered a few words, like I was trying to figure out what it meant, and then simply repeated the same thing I'd heard my cousin tell a customer, explaining how this line meant she'd have a long life, how this meant she'd find love, and the usual nonsense people loved to hear.

Of course, this only excited more of them, and I didn't manage to get out of there until I'd had to make up some outlandish fortunes and been given a bag of more money than I'd ever seen.

As heavy as it was on its own, my tray was so light now that I was practically skipping on the road home. I'd have to come back the next day. I'd always stuck to poorer areas, where it seemed like people would be more interested, but I'd apparently been overlooking an under-served market, and I would not do that again.

The coins in my blouse were enough for everyone. We wouldn't have to worry for weeks. They were going to be thrilled. There'd probably be a party in my honor.

I chuckled, the grin no longer enough to express my joy. Everything was perfect.

I turned down the road. It wasn't dark or empty. There were plenty of people on it, but they were wealthier, and I was well below any of their notice. Home was only an hour's walk away, maybe forty minutes at the rate I was going, so I wasn't overly worried.

But one of them started following me.

It was an older man, with gray hair, a frock coat, and a cane that rang out on the cobblestones. It was what first made me notice him.

The sound hadn't meant anything at first. People had walking sticks, and they made noise; it was no different than anything else I'd hear on the road, like footsteps, hoofbeats, and shouted slurs. But unlike all of the other noises, it didn't go away as I kept walking.

I didn't want to look, but it kept thudding, never getting any farther away.

He was keeping pace with me. I tried speeding up, pretending I was still skipping merrily along. For a moment, the sound grew fainter, and I thought maybe I'd been paranoid over nothing, but then it got closer again.

It kept thudding. Beat. Beat. Every few steps, never growing any farther.

I risked a look back and saw the proper older man in a frock coat. Nothing about him seemed interesting. He didn't even react when I looked. But he was the exact same distance he'd been when I'd first noticed him.

A pit formed in my stomach. I tried turning off to a different road, but it didn't change. That same sound kept following me at the same distance.

Could he have been the owner of that house? Maybe he thought I stole something? Was that why he was following me?

I turned again, and it stayed exactly as far away. It just kept coming. No matter what I did, he was following me, and I'd been dumb enough to turn into a village street I didn't know as well.

I'd been here a few months earlier. The houses were all wooden, with thatch roofs, and sides that seemed ready to cave in, with tarps in places to keep out the draft. There were people on the roads, as evidenced by one spitting at my feet, but I didn't know anyone here. There were no other Rroms I could turn to or anyplace I could go.

Part of me wanted to try knocking on a door to sell something, but standing in one place with him behind me felt like a terrible decision.

But I had to do something.

I turned back onto the main road, and he didn't stop me, but when I looked back, I swear he was the slightest bit closer. Nowhere near arm's reach, still a good ten paces away, but he'd been farther before, hadn't he?

I kept walking. I was maybe half an hour from home after that detour. I could make it.

He was only eight paces away now. What was he trying to do? Why hadn't he said anything? "Is there something you want?" I finally asked, turning, trying to smile but knowing the fear took it from me.

His eyes finally met mine. They were cold, lifeless things that somehow still seemed to show joy at the look on my face. "Good evening," he said.

I glanced up at the sky. The sun was barely hitting the horizon. Evening seemed a bit early, but if the worst he was going to do was be wrong about the time, then I could hardly complain. "Good evening," I repeated, not wanting to correct him. "Do I know you?"

His teeth showed in a mockery of a smile. They were white, straight, and far too sharp. "No, I don't believe you do."

I took a step back.

His cane echoed again as he stepped toward me, seeming to cross the entire distance between us in a single step. "It is a lovely night for a walk, isn't it?"

I opened my mouth, but no words came out. A lump seemed to have formed in my throat, and I couldn't force anything past it.

"Oh, it's quite all right." His finger pressed against my lips. "You don't need to say anything more. Ever again, in fact."

I snapped on his finger hard enough that the bone crunched, and blood sprayed into my mouth. It popped free, and I felt the vile digit loose in my mouth, rolling against my throat and only adding to how badly I wanted to vomit as I swung my tray at his head, jars and toys flying off and smashing on the ground.

He caught it. "Oh, I do wish you hadn't done that." He yanked the tray from my hand with so little effort, I might as well have been a rag doll. He snapped it over his knee, then flung it to the side. "We were playing a simple game, and you had to ruin it." He stared at his missing finger, then picked me up by the throat.

It was the strangest thing I'd ever felt. It hurt, of course, like nothing had ever hurt before as his fingers crushed my windpipe, and I gasped for air, but he was holding me in the air in a single hand. I'd compared myself to a doll, but I hadn't realized how true it was. Whatever this monster was, I was merely another toy to play with.

He pressed against my broken trachea as I tried to scream, but nothing came out except his finger, and it fell to the ground. Those fangs he had for teeth sank into my throat, and I knew I was going to die. I reached under my shirt, feeling the bag of coins but moved past it. I knew I still had it. I had to. I wouldn't have lost it.

My hand clasped the hilt of the knife my cousin had given me. It was little more than a letter opener, but it was all I had. I drew it and stabbed into his chest, and blood sprayed out with so much force, I could taste it.

I thought he'd at least be surprised enough to drop me, but he only tightened his grip, and the world went black as I finally dropped to the ground.

That was how I died. The first vampire I'd ever met stalked me and tormented me, then left me dead on the side of the road.

But I'd tasted his blood. He hadn't meant for it to happen, but it was enough to make sure I didn't stay dead. I was quite possibly the first vampire to ever accidentally become one, but at the time, all I knew was that I'd been attacked and left for dead on the side of the road. I had no idea that I'd become the same sort of monster that had killed me.

CHAPTER ELEVEN

Dorenia

"That's not possible," Kalila says.

"What isn't?"

"You can't…no one is turned like that. Vampires choose to do it. I've been hunting them for over a decade, and I've never heard of anything like this happening. It doesn't make sense. He should've been fast enough to avoid any of that. You're lying."

I need her to believe me. What can I possibly do to get through to her? "I'm not."

"Then why are you wasting my time with this?"

"I need you to understand who he is and what he can do. He's a serious threat, and you don't want to go in blind." It's the best way to pitch it. The story is obviously to get her sympathy, but if I treat it like a tactical necessity, maybe she'll keep listening long enough for the truth to sink in.

She crosses her arms and sits back but doesn't say anything. I take it as a sign to continue.

I woke up on the side of the road, the sun well below the horizon. I felt my belly to find the bag of coins still there. No one must've wanted to touch me. Their loss.

I felt my throat, expecting the same pain as before, but it seemed whole and unbroken. There wasn't even a tear where his teeth had bit in. I tried speaking, and a noise came out. "I'm all right?" I asked no one and received no answer.

My tray was still broken on the ground, and blood still clung to my face and blouse. It hadn't been a dream or any sort of hallucination. I was attacked. I was killed. But I was fine.

I rubbed my throat, knowing that there had to be an injury, that something had to be wrong, but it was perfect. It was like nothing had ever happened.

I pulled myself to my feet and ignored my fallen goods. I'd made enough money that it wasn't a huge loss.

Home was so close. All I had to do was walk, but as I began moving, I felt a pain in my belly. At first, I thought it was an injury I'd overlooked, but as I began licking my lips, I realized that I was starving.

I hadn't eaten all day, so that made sense. Someone back home would probably have saved me some food. It should give me the motivation to make the walk.

But as a woman walked by, I found myself staring at her neck, unable to look away. She smelled more delicious than any food I'd ever smelled. It was like a succulent roast mixed with the most flavorful wine, but somehow more than that. I was drooling.

I tried to fight back, to keep from moving toward her, but she was already within arm's reach.

She turned to me, shock and revulsion clear on her face. "Get away from me, gy—"

My teeth sank into her.

I blinked, barely managing to keep from pulling away and taking her neck with me. What was I doing? Why was I doing this? I released her and stepped back, licking my lips and barely managing not to moan at the taste. She ran, and I had to fight every instinct to chase her.

What the hell was going on with me?

I wiped my face and rubbed at the blood on my shirt. It was too dry to come off, but I needed to get rid of it. What was I? I had to look like a monster, and it didn't seem far off from the truth.

That man, that thing that attacked me. Was I like him now? He had bitten me and left me for dead. Why was I like him? What was he?

Maybe someone back home could tell me. All I could do was keep from hurting anyone. I had enough money to help out, and they'd hide me if that woman ran to the police. We'd probably have to leave town sooner than I'd imagined, but at least we wouldn't do so penniless.

In mere minutes, I was there. I looked around in confusion. It had been farther than this. I thought back to how even as I ran, he was always right behind me. Was this part of that too?

I wanted to talk to someone, to ask what was happening to me, but I couldn't do it while looking like this. I headed for my wagon only for someone to start calling my name. The words were loud and rang in my ears, but I turned to face the one who said it. Her image was so sharp that I couldn't recognize her at first, but she coalesced into my cousin, Mala.

"God, Dorenia, you look like hell."

"I'm fine," I lied. I only wanted to get cleaned up, to not have them all see me looking like a monster.

"You're covered in blood. What happened to you?"

"It's nothing." I shook my head and tried to move around her, but she grabbed my arm, her pleading eyes meeting mine.

"Dorenia, what happened? Did someone hurt you?"

I shook my head.

Her grip tightened. It was nothing like his. She was so weak. So human. Unlike whatever I was now. "You're covered in blood and coming home well after midnight. You're not leaving without answering me."

I sighed. Was it really that late? How long had I lay on the side of the road? "Fine, I'll tell you, but can we please go to my wagon? I want to get cleaned up."

She held my gaze for a long moment but finally nodded. "All right. I'll fetch some water, but as soon as I get there, you're telling me everything."

I did. She helped me clean off, and I told her every detail of what had happened, from how he'd followed me, to how I'd bitten off his finger, to how I'd died and woken up hours later in the dirt.

"What the hell?" she finally asked when it was all done. Because she, unlike some people, was capable of not interrupting a story.

"I don't know." I sobbed. Tears had blocked my vision halfway through the story. I tried to wipe them away, but they kept coming. "He's turned me into something. After I woke up, I…" I trailed off. Could I truly say it? How would she ever look at me again? "I attacked someone. I was so hungry. I needed her blood. I bit her throat, but when I saw what I'd done, I released her, and she ran away, screaming. She's probably gone to the police already to say that one of us attacked her."

"Shit. Okay, don't tell anyone else about this. They always say we've attacked them. Stay in here, and I'll ask around and see what I can find out."

I followed her advice. The next day, police came, beating people, asking questions, demanding what we'd been up to, and I heard every second of it while I hid in my home, not willing to risk facing them. I felt like a coward, but Mala was right. If the woman could identify me, it would only make matters worse. And until we knew what I was, there was little we could do for it.

That night, Mala knocked on my door, and I let her in. She wouldn't meet my eyes and seemed unwilling to speak.

"Mala, what is it?"

She shook her head, tears falling. "You attacked someone, Dorenia."

My heart dropped. I knew what she was going to say.

"They're talking about kicking you out of the caravan. Tsura is saying that you sound like a strigoi, an undead monster that feeds on blood. I told her she was wrong, but with what you said, I don't think she is."

"I didn't mean to be…" What a pointless thing to say. When had my desires ever mattered?

"I know." She blinked away tears and threw her arms around me. "I'm so sorry, Dorenia."

I hugged back, my tears falling onto her shoulder. "It's okay. I don't want to bring harm to all of you."

"It's still not fair. You don't deserve this."

I nodded, but it was hard to agree. I'd attacked someone. I could've killed her. This was precisely what I deserved. "Did she say anything else about strigoi?" I asked, pulling away.

"Only that they're corpses that rise at night to feed on the living, and supposedly, they can turn into animals. Can you do that?"

"I haven't tried."

She chuckled. "You could turn into a cat and stay in my wagon. Then you wouldn't have to leave."

I imagined myself as a cat, but my body didn't seem to do anything. "I don't think I can."

"I figured. But it sounds like you need to drink blood fairly often or else you could get dangerous. She did say one other thing. I didn't want to mention it, as it was rather mean, but she said that you were too much of a risk to keep here, that if you didn't feed regularly, you'd lose control and be unable to keep from eating your family."

I nodded. "That sounds like what happened before."

"All right."

I stared at her. "What?"

She brushed her hair back and smiled at me. "You need to eat. If we're kicking you out of the caravan, I'm not sending you out there starving. You're my best friend, and you're still family, no matter what they decide—though it sounds like they've already decided—so eat."

"You don't mean…"

"I do. I trust you. You won't kill me. Drink enough to satisfy you. You can have more whenever you need. I know you'll always be able to find me. That way, we can keep people safe."

I wanted to say no, to insist that it wasn't worth it, that I'd end up killing her, but before I could form any of the words, my teeth were in her throat. I hugged her, moaning into her neck as I drank her life, the flavor the most intoxicating thing I'd ever encountered. Nothing could compare to it; it was like the ambrosia of myth. I knew that I'd never be able to stop. That she'd die, and I wouldn't even care. I'd just keep drinking from everyone until there was nothing left.

I could see my family dead at my feet, and I knew it would happen. If there had been any doubt that they were right to expel me, it was gone.

I managed to release her, panting.

She covered her neck with her hand, but she didn't recoil from me. I didn't deserve that kindness. "Do you feel better?"

I nodded, unable to take my eyes off her. I needed more. I wanted to keep drinking until it was all gone.

"Whenever you need. Though give me a few days to recover first."

I wasn't willing to open my mouth lest it latch on to her again.

She smiled at me. "I'm going to try to talk them into letting you stay. You're not a danger."

I shook my head. It was all I could manage.

"You stopped yourself from killing me and that girl, when you knew what leaving her alive would cost you. That should be enough to convince them. Just wait. I'll manage. You won't have to leave."

"It's too dangerous," I finally said.

She rolled her eyes. "As the food here, I think I get to decide what's too dangerous. You're family. We're not turning on you simply because someone attacked you. None of this is your fault."

I sighed and leaned against the wall, trying to keep myself from biting her again. I reached into my shirt on the floor and pulled out the money. "You all need this. I should leave. I can take care of myself now. There's no reason to bring it onto our family."

"And you think there's any chance that they won't blame us anyway?"

I pursed my lips.

"Dorenia, as far as they're concerned, we're all the same. Whether you're out there or in here, you'll be treated as one of us by everyone else. You didn't do anything wrong. And especially when you come home with enough to feed everyone for..." She took the purse. "Goddamn."

"I found a better place to sell."

"Then stay. You can keep doing that, and we won't have to worry about food anymore. And since you don't need to eat, we can take your needs off the table."

I glared at her.

She smirked. "I'm plenty for you. But fine, you can still have supplies too, I guess, if you must receive anything from your money."

I crossed my arms and rolled my eyes but couldn't help but smile.

"That's better. Not talking about how you need to leave now."

"It's still the better option."

"No, it isn't. You're just trying to sacrifice yourself for everyone else, like you always do. So I'm going to go tell them to shove it and that you're family. With any luck, they'll understand, and you'll get to stay. If not, I guess I'll go with you, and we can find someplace new to live."

"You're not—"

She held up her hand. "It's my decision. And I've made it. You're family, Dorenia. And I'm not losing you."

Without another word, she strode out of my wagon, and I could hear her chewing out the elder from across the camp. It was a miracle that he didn't throw us both out, but somehow, she *convinced him to let me stay, and the next day, I went out selling my goods like any other day.*

"What does any of this have to do with him?" Kalila snaps. "I assume it's the guy who turned you, right? Now I know. I don't need to know everything that happened after."

She needed to know that I haven't killed people and that I have family. "I'm getting to it. He's coming back into the story, don't worry. I can't skip to it. I'd rather not go straight from the worst thing that ever happened to me to the second one."

She huffs but lets me keep going.

It was uneventful. The sun was bright and unpleasant, but beyond making me squint and itch where it hit my exposed flesh, not much had changed. We hit the richer part of Liverpool again and made easy money almost like before, only this time, no one tried to murder us on the way back. Though, I suppose "tried" would suggest he'd failed, and my heart didn't seem to be beating anymore.

The next few days, we kept going like that, and everything was perfect. We were making more money than our family could've imagined, and anytime I grew hungry, I had food, even though the knowledge that if I ever went too far, that food would die, and I'd lose my dearest friend, ate at me as much as I ate her.

Around a week later, however, when Mala came to get me, I could barely move. "What's wrong?" she asked.

I stared at her and forced myself to sit up. I was in my bed in my wagon, and it felt like I was lying in a pit of spikes. "I…"

She took my hand. "Do you need blood? You fed last night. Are you getting hungrier? I can ask someone else."

I shook my head. "I don't think…it's that." The words were torture to get out. "It's like I'm falling apart inside. Maybe death finally caught up with me."

Mala stared at me, biting her lip and looking behind her as if she couldn't bring herself to abandon me.

"It's okay."

She nodded. "I'll get Tsura. She might know something."

I could hear her calling through the camp. They ran back, their echoing footsteps ringing in my head and making it throb. I closed my eyes. The meager light through my curtains was too much. The sounds were too much. Moving was far too much. I lay there, willing the pain to go away even if it meant I had to die again.

Steps thudded on the wooden floor as the two of them entered. "Dorenia, what seems to be the matter?" Tsura's voice came.

I tried to open my eyes but couldn't. "It hurts."

"What hurts?" She sounded concerned.

"Everything. I feel like I'm dying again."

I could feel her looking me over, leaning above me, searching for an answer. "Has anything changed? What could've prompted this? Have you fed?"

"She ate last night," Mala answered.

"Then what's different?"

I tried to shrug and failed. "I didn't do anything. I came home last night, had a bit of soup—and Mala—and washed my bedding and went to sleep."

"Could it be the soup?" Mala asked. "Maybe there was something in it that strigoi can't eat?"

"That's possible," she muttered and made a contemplative noise. "Had you cleaned your bedding before then?"

"Once a week, all my life."

"I meant since you became a strigoi."

"Oh." I wanted to stare at her, to cock my head, to blink, to react in some way other than with a pained groan, but that was all I could manage. "I don't think I had."

I could picture her sitting there, stroking her chin, staring at the curtain of my window like she could see out of it as she went over the myths in her head and what they could mean. "I've heard it said that strigoi have to sleep in the dirt where they were buried."

"I wasn't buried."

"But you were left on the side of the road. Tell us where."

Where had it been? I'd left that village and turned back toward home. That was where he'd grabbed me, wasn't it? "It was on the main road. There's a village I'd been to only once before, maybe half an hour from here, and it was just past that, toward here."

"Maybe there'll still be evidence of your fight?" Mala said. "Unless you can be more specific."

I tried to shake my head but only managed to move it the barest inch.

Mala ran from the wagon, and Tsura followed her, walking slowly. I lay there in agony, barely able to move and knowing that without that dirt, there was nothing I could do.

When Mala came back hours later, she had pockets full of different dirt, and we used all of them. It felt gross, and I woke up dirtier than when I went to bed, but it worked. We managed to narrow it down over time and not make so much of a mess, I didn't wake up in pain anymore and could function exactly like I used to, but faster and stronger and with an insatiable need for blood.

For years, other than sleeping in dirt, drinking Mala, and eventually another cousin's blood every few days, it was like nothing had changed. We worked, we ate together, we had parties and evenings drinking. If it wasn't for the fact that I could smell every human for the better part of a mile, I'd have thought it was all a dream. Until I saw him again.

CHAPTER TWELVE

Dorenia

"Okay, so it's the bastard who turned you," Kalila says. "He's trying to finish the job. I get it. We can go kill him now."

"Let me finish the story," I snap. "You need to hear it all. I don't want us to walk in without being fully ready."

"I don't see what more I could need to know."

"Well, listen, and you'll find out."

We walked on the road home. I could've easily run it, but the one time I tried carrying Mala, she threw up, so we'd been enjoying evening walks home together each night. "You know, you don't have to keep coming with me," I said, as we walked along the river. It was only a little off the road, and it both avoided crowds and gave us a better view.

She didn't quite meet my eyes as she shrugged. "I know."

"You're still worried I'll eat someone."

"No!" she said far too loudly. "Maybe a little. But not really. I trust you. I'm more worried for you. I know how much it affected you when you attacked that girl. It's not that I think you're going to bring shame to our family or get us kicked out of Liverpool, though I'm sure we'll manage that anyway. It's that I'm scared that you'll find yourself in a position where you can't resist it again. Maybe you won't kill anyone, but it's still a temptation that I don't want you to have to face alone. If I'm there with you, then you don't have to."

I tossed a stone on the river, and it bounced a few dozen times. "I don't know if I would. I'd like to think I wouldn't. It only happened the one time, and that was when I'd come back to life and was starving. You've made sure I haven't gotten to that point again."

"And I'll never let you."

I glanced at her, trying to give an appreciative smile, but fear kept it from me. "I know that you'd like to do your own work." It sounded almost petulant. I was trying to avoid saying that I didn't want to burden her when I already took so much.

"As much as we're making and as little work as it is, I'd take this any day. And it means I get to spend time with you. If anything, you're doing me a favor."

"All right." I stared at my feet. The path was even enough that even without my improved balance, I wouldn't need to watch my step, but it gave me an excuse to avoid her eyes. "Do you think I'm doing something to our customers? You're right, we've been making a lot of money. Too much. I can give them any price, and I barely have to pitch it, and they open up their purses and buy anything we offer. Hell, they buy our cloth when they have far nicer fabric."

She took my hand and stood next to me. "I hadn't considered that. Or maybe I hadn't wanted to."

I nodded. "You think I am?"

"Maybe. Is it so wrong if you are? They have money. And it's quality goods. We're hardly ripping them off."

"Are you making excuses?"

She squeezed my hand but didn't say anything as we resumed our leisurely pace.

"Am I still the same person?" I asked. "I died. Or maybe she died."

"You're you. You're Dorenia. Worry about the morality all you want, but don't you dare think that I don't know my best friend. You're not some monster wearing her face, you're my cousin, you're the same girl I've been playing with since we were born. I would know you anywhere, and you're you."

I nodded and rubbed my eyes with my free hand, trying not to cry. "Thank you."

She took in a breath as if she had more to say, but instead, she only smiled at me and tugged on my arm for me to pick up speed. "It's getting dark. And cold."

"I could always carry you."

"No!"

I chuckled. That felt more like it. "Let's go back on the road. It'll be faster."

She nodded, and we moved back to the trail. It was late enough that there weren't many people around, so we had free rein and managed to pick up the pace, not quite running down the main road.

We slowed as we saw someone on the path so we could go around them, but as we got closer, if there was blood in my veins, it would've run cold.

There was a man in a fancy suit, with a top hat and a cane. He was old, far older than I remembered, though perhaps his strength erased his age in my mind. He strolled down the road, looking around, sniffing the air. He must've caught the scent of a young woman, as he turned, his eyes alight with hunger, the same look I saw on them the better part of a year earlier and the same look my victim must've seen that night.

His eyes met mine, and he faltered.

"Dorenia?" Mala asked, sounding pained. "You're crushing my hand."

I stared down at it. Her fingers would bruise, but they weren't broken.

"Dorenia," he repeated after her.

She looked between us.

"How are you still alive?" He sniffed the air again, his face contorting from that look of hunger to one of anger. "How did you become a vampire?"

I took a step back, dragging Mala with me.

"Oh! Oh." She stared at him. "He's the man who—"

"My reputation precedes me. How interesting. I've never had a victim live to tell the tale before. I should fix that." He strode toward us, his cane thudding on the ground.

I picked Mala up and ran. She yelped and clung to me as I barreled down the road, narrowly avoiding knocking over someone else. I stopped and looked back. It was an older woman looking around confused and jostled. If he was still following us, he'd go right for her. She'd be vulnerable and in the way, and it would be my fault. "Mala, go home."

"The hell I will. I'm not leaving you to deal with this monster."

I spun on her, but what could I say? He knew what he was doing. Beyond running, I hadn't tested any of my new abilities. I could still remember the feeling of his hand crushing my neck. It'd happen again. Would it kill me this time? Could I die if I wasn't staked into a coffin I'd never been given? Where was his coffin?

"We can run," she said. "We have enough money. If we talk to everyone, they'll be ready to leave. We don't have to stay in Liverpool with this...I probably shouldn't keep saying monster."

"I'd like to think that I'm not, but he definitely is."

"Get," the woman shouted. "I see the way you're looking at me. I don't have any money on me."

Mala met my eyes. "He wants to kill you. I doubt he'll go for her, and if he does, I'm not sure she doesn't deserve it."

"But—"

"Get!" the old woman repeated. "I'll call the constable."

I sniffed. There was the sickening scent of death in the air. He was nearby. He must've been intentionally staying back like he did before; he wanted us to be scared. The old lady had already seen me run, so there was no sense in hiding it. I grabbed Mala again and ran all the way home. It was a terrible idea. All it would do was lead him right to us, but it wasn't as if he couldn't find us on his own.

I stopped in the middle of our caravan, and Mala leapt from my hands, looking green. "We have to get out of here," she shouted.

Our chief looked up from a card game a few wagons over. "What's going on?" he asked as he approached us.

"The guy that killed her is coming for us," Mala said.

"We don't know that."

"You don't think him looking at me like food and saying that he wanted to kill you was a pretty good clue? He's coming for us, and we can either bury our heads in the sand, or we can leave. It's what we do. We've angered enough people here. It's time to find someplace else. Preferably without an angry strigoi who wants to kill all of us."

That scent was growing closer. His cane sounded far away, but it was there. Thud. Thud. Growing closer. "He's already here."

"Everyone, hitch up the horses," Mala shouted.

The camp began to move all at once. No one tried to argue. We formed up the wagons and readied the horses, but it wouldn't be fast enough. He was there, right outside, waiting for us, but for what? Did he want to catch us as we fled? Was he waiting for when we fell asleep, and he wasn't expecting us to leave?

No, as loud as we were, he'd have heard us. He was trying to manipulate me, to make me too scared and cause me to do something stupid. So I did something stupid, and I just had to hope it wasn't what he wanted because nothing else I could think of would work. "I need a weapon."

Tsura tossed me a woodcutting axe. I hadn't even realized she was nearby. She must have wanted to impart some more wisdom. "Take his head. If anything will kill him, it's that." It was useful.

"Don't be ridiculous," Mala said. "You don't know how to fight."

"I know a little."

"We're running. That's it."

I jabbed the axe toward the road. "He's waiting out there, watching us. As soon as we leave, he'll kill us all. The least I can do is buy time."

"Yeah, and sacrifice yourself again."

I shook my head. "I won't."

"If you don't come back..."

I hugged her. "I promise, I'll come back. If I can kill him, great, he deserves it, he murdered me, but all I need is to keep him busy while you all leave. I'll meet you partway to—"

"Don't say it out loud," our chief said. "If you think he's watching."

"You're right. But we're still going where we'd planned?"

"The one after that. That one was too close. I know how fast you are."

I looked to the road, but he still hadn't come any closer. "You truly think that's any better?"

"I don't know, but I know it can't be worse."

He was right. I sighed and tightened my grip on the axe. I could travel around a mile a minute without pushing myself. Even with his cane, I couldn't assume he'd be any slower. Sheffield was at least a day's ride away, but either of us could run it in an hour, easily. How would I keep something like him busy? Could I lead him on a wild-goose chase? Nothing seemed like it would work well enough, but I didn't have the luxury of planning. I had to act now if I wanted my family to be safe.

I took a deep breath and stepped away from the camp.

"Wait," Mala said. "Do you need some blood first?"

I licked my lips, looking to her neck, then back to the road. Would that attract him?

"I don't know what you're getting yourself into, so please, let me do what little I can to help."

I didn't have the strength to resist, and I promptly bit into her neck. It had only been a day since I'd last fed, so I kept myself from going too far, only allowing a snack, but I had to hope it was enough. I was going to need everything I had to stand a chance against him.

He was out there. I could smell him. I'd had practice tracking, but that was the occasional runaway chicken, not undead monsters who could be somewhere else as quickly as they wanted. If he didn't want to be found, I wasn't sure I could do anything about it.

But he wanted to kill me. And more than that, he wanted to scare me or else he wouldn't have done the whole show of stalking me and watching my family. Running from me would ruin that mystique and turn him from predator into prey.

The scent of death was close. He didn't smell like a corpse, but it clung to him, not overpowering but simply there. He wasn't on the main road, but he didn't seem far from it. As I walked toward the river, the scent grew closer. He was no longer keeping up his cat-and-mouse game of always being the same distance away. Was he that eager to end this?

The axe felt heavy. I'd never killed anyone before. I wasn't sure I could do it, but I knew that if I didn't at least try, then he'd kill the people I loved. All I had to do was buy time, but if I wasn't willing to give it my all and actually try to kill him, then I wouldn't stand a chance, as he certainly wouldn't be holding back.

I found him waiting by the river, sitting on a rock, his gaze locked in the direction of our caravan. Could he see it from there? My vision was enhanced by the change, but I had trouble imagining that I'd be able to make anything out at this distance. I wanted to turn and check, but that would mean turning my back on him, and that wasn't worth the risk.

He stood as I approached, his eyes narrowing, fangs showing in a look of utter disgust. It wasn't exactly a look I was unaccustomed to seeing, particularly on those as wealthy as he appeared. "How did you do it?" he asked. "I didn't make you. How are you alive? You were human when I ate you."

It bothered him. I knew he hated that I was alive. That look when he first saw me had made it clear. He didn't understand it, and that seemed to drive him crazy. I could use that. In a proper fight, I didn't like my odds against someone who had been doing this for a lot longer than me, but in a conversation, I was fairly certain I could manage. I was there to buy time, and if that meant answering his questions, then he could ask away. "You called me a vampire earlier. I thought I was a strigoi."

"It's not a meaningful distinction," he said, tapping his cane on the ground. It wasn't in the normal threatening manner; it seemed more irritated. It was working. He was getting caught up already. Maybe he wouldn't notice my family leaving. "A strigoi is a type of vampire. Or maybe another word for it. We're an old creature, and I've never been quite certain if there were different similar species or if it simply manifested that differently sometimes. It seems to change for everyone."

"What's it like for you?"

His eyes narrowed. Was I being too obvious? "You truly expect me to give away my inner workings and weaknesses? You won't be alive long enough for any of it to matter. You're a mistake. An impossibility. And as curious as that is, do not for a second think that my curiosity will allow you to live."

"Well, if I'm going to die anyway, then what's the harm? But can I really die? Aren't I already dead?"

His eyes narrowed, but he folded his hands on the top of his cane and said, "In a manner of speaking, yes, you're dead. You died the night that I killed you. But you're not exactly a corpse now, are you? You're standing right in front of me and look alive enough for me to kill you again. It's funny, I've never gotten to kill the same woman twice. I'll savor that."

Every instinct told me to just swing my axe right then. He wouldn't be expecting it. I wasn't sure I had it in me to kill, but if it meant saving my family, I was at least willing to try. But if I failed, I would have barely bought any time, and even taking him by surprise, I didn't expect it to work. "But how was I made? How are vampires, we, made?"

He sighed and shook his head, his cane tapping harder, sending dirt flying up. "While I've never made another before, and greatly regret that you were my first, we drink someone's blood and let them drink ours. It has to be enough to kill them, our blood should be the only blood in them, but I'm not sure if it has to be literal or if it's a metaphorical thing. I simply know that it tends to work."

"Tends to? It can fail?"

"Sometimes. I've been around long enough to have heard of it, though I've never seen it myself."

I nodded like it was the most interesting thing I'd ever heard. I didn't care much about monsters or how they worked. I wanted to know more about me, but he was the last person I would ask about that. "Then how was I made?" I remembered his finger, and his blood spraying me as I stabbed him. The taste had been vile, like concentrated evil, but apparently, it was the only reason I was still alive…or what passed for it.

"I don't know." His voice was scarcely more than a growl, and he bared his fangs, the very teeth that had torn my throat open. The sight scared me but not like I expected it to. When he'd killed me, I'd been more terrified than I'd ever been in my entire life. I was scared now, facing him, with the lives of everyone I loved on the line, but I didn't feel traumatized. I knew I might die, that it was maybe more likely than not, and I knew that if I did, he'd kill them as well. That scared me. But seeing the last thing now that I'd seen before I'd died didn't make me relive that trauma; it only made me sure that I couldn't let my family go through the same thing. He was a monster, and as loath as I was to take a life, if I could, it was my duty to, and there was probably no one else in the whole world who could.

I swung the axe.

His cane flew up to block. That was exactly what I expected, which if I knew how to fight, should've meant that I was feinting and was going to come from another angle, but I'd put all my strength into that swing, hoping I could take his head, so it struck the cane full force with the shaft. If it had at least been the head, I'd have shortened his weapon, but he was a lot better than I was.

I pulled my axe free and leapt back, but he didn't give me time to regroup. He rushed forward, darting his cane out, and I barely managed to knock it away, only for his fist to slam into my gut. I fell to my knees, and the cane struck me in the jaw. My world spun.

"I don't know why you're still trying to fight. You know you're overpowered. You're a child and one of lower stock at that. I have been at this for centuries. You come with an axe, expecting to take my head." He spat, sounding more disgusted than angry. "I will kill you again. And I will make it slow."

I pushed off the ground, and he rushed me to strike with the cane again, so I let him hit me. I could take as much pain as I needed. All that mattered was stopping him from coming after us. I brought my axe down on his leg, taking it clean off while his hit only sent my head ringing and spattered blood everywhere.

He screamed. I'd never been one for hurting others, but it was hard not to enjoy his pain. The world seemed to have dimmed some. I tried blinking and found my right eye didn't seem to be working. I followed with another swing, but he leapt back.

I probably could have killed him then. Maybe. Possibly. Even with him missing a leg, I wasn't certain I could win, but I knew that running felt like the worst option, even as I took it. Maybe I was scared, or maybe I felt that I'd done enough.

He chased me, and I let him. Every time I got too far away, I'd sniff him out and make sure I was close enough. I stayed away from people, trying to keep by the river. Whenever he started to approach the city, I'd charge him, and his scent would grow farther away. He wanted to kill me, but he'd need to feed to heal, and if he tried, I stopped him. For the first time since we'd met, he was scared. I wouldn't let him eat. At the time, I hadn't been sure if feeding would fix a wound that bad, but I knew it couldn't make the situation better for me.

I spent the entire day at that game, tormenting him as he had me but avoiding an actual fight. Finally, when my family had time to be well out of reach, I slipped away the next time he went toward humans. I couldn't manage to kill him, and I have no idea how many more suffered because of that.

When I made it to Sheffield, Mala panicked at the state of my face and gave me blood, and life went back to normal. We'd made it away clean, even if I knew he'd be coming back for us.

CHAPTER THIRTEEN

"We kept that up for generations," Dorenia says. "Every few years, he'd catch up to us, I'd distract him, and we'd get away. It seemed incredible, but it kept working. It was just never enough. He got a few people over the years, family, children, people who meant the world to me, but I could never manage to kill him. I tried so many times. I practiced for years, but I was never good enough.

"Finally, I couldn't put the children I'd watched grow old in danger any longer. I set out on my own. It made blood harder to find, but I never killed for it, and I checked in on my family often. He seemed intent on finding me. I kept on the move, keeping our meetings to every decade or so. Once I fled to the other side of the ocean, it seemed like it was finally over. I've been here for over a century now, and every source I had confirmed that he still hadn't found me or tracked down my family, as I still talk to them every week, and they're fine. But last week, he finally caught up to me. I have more resources and the means to put up a fight, but apparently, he's grown with the times as well. He's been in town, asking about me. I've tried to put out some false information, but he sent these vampires to kill me, to get rid of the monster he accidentally created, and he'll send more next time. I'll happily help you take care of your villain. From everything I've heard, he sounds as dreadful as mine, but I'll be dead if we don't take care of this one first."

I stare at her. I didn't expect her life story. From any other vampire, I'd want to kill her for the inconvenience, but she isn't a killer. I don't want to believe her, to trust that yet another vampire is somehow a better person than I am, but I can see it in her eyes. She's less of a monster than I am, which worryingly seems to often be the case, and she needs my help. And more importantly, I need hers. "You seriously didn't kill anyone when you first turned? I managed to keep it to a soldier, someone who'd killed my friends and neighbors, but I still had to drain him dry." Can there really be two vampires who've never killed a human in this city? At least, there can't be more than that. It would be impossible. There's no way any of the others I've killed could be innocent too. I won't believe it.

"Maybe it's because I knew what it was like to be on the other end."

"I did too."

A flash of guilt shows on her face. "I'm sorry, I didn't mean it like that. Will you tell me your story?"

"No. We have a vampire to kill." At least that one is a killer.

She smirks, and it's still a strangely lovely smile, for a vampire. Her fangs are barely visible, pressing against her lower lip. "We have a deal?"

"We had a deal before you told me that story. Even if I wasn't happy to kill another vampiric asshole like this fucker, you kinda have me over a barrel here. You know where he is, and I don't."

"I suppose I do. There are worse places I could have you." She giggles, giving me a look that I hate to admit could pass for lascivious.

I sigh. I should've known better than to phrase it like that. The whole point was to distance myself further from a vampire I am already feeling sympathetic for—and when I'd managed to do the same a little while ago with Mia—but clearly, a minor vulgarity isn't enough for that when she already knows I'm helping her. "Do you know where he is? Your guy. I already know you know where mine is." I wish I could at least blame her for keeping it secret, but she's fearing for her life. I've never met a vampire so hard to hate.

"I don't precisely know where Reynolds is. I know he's looking for you, and I can arrange a meeting."

"And you'll do that once we kill your guy? Does he have a name?" I need to focus on the kill. Maybe it'll turn out she was lying about everything, and then I'll be able to kill her after the deal. She's an information broker and has dealings with that disgusting bazaar. She's not a good person. She can't be. She's a monster. Who, if she's telling the truth, has never killed a human, and spent a century looking after the people she loves. Part of me hates her for it. It's better than I ever managed. It makes me feel like I really am a monster.

She shakes her head. "He never told me one, and from everything I've learned over the years, he's used a number of different aliases. I have no idea if any of them are his real name. However, I do know that he's staying at the Hilton in the honeymoon suite."

"With a handful of goons, I assume?"

That smirk appears again, her dark brown eyes glinting with mirth. "Around a dozen, though they're likely not in the actual bedroom if you want to go in through the window."

"I'd rather take them all head-on. Trying for a surprise attack against vampires tends to mean they all rush in to back him up, and the ambush turns into being overwhelmed. I'm far more comfortable fighting in the hallway where they can't get as far. The elevator doesn't go right to the suite, does it?"

"It doesn't. The suite is at the end of the hallway."

"Perfect. Do you have more people, or is it only me?"

"I'm coming with you."

I look her up and down. She carries that claymore like she knows what she's doing with it, but I've never teamed up with a vampire before, and the idea leaves a bad taste in my mouth.

"Don't even think about it," she says. "I don't know what bullshit you're about to say, probably something about me being a monster, judging by everything they say about you, but I already saved your life once today. You're my best shot at making it out of this alive. If you die because you're too stupid to accept my help killing my own nemesis, we both die."

I cross my arms. "Fine," I mutter.

"You don't have to trust me—"

"It's not that. Not exactly." She's far too easy to trust. Experience tells me that it's a trick, but I can't manage to believe that.

"The vampire hunter who lies about being a vampire and couldn't go a single visit to the Community Center without murdering someone and getting kicked out doesn't distrust me for being a vampire?"

I shrug. "I do. Of course I do. You're a monster. But from everything you've said, you're not much of one."

"That's why I told you my story. I know your reputation, and if you didn't know the truth about me, you'd probably take my head as soon as you finished saving my life."

"Probably."

"Then why believe me?"

"I like to think I know when someone's lying to me. Like how I was pretty sure there wasn't actually anything to learn in your story, and you apparently only told it to get my mercy. I hadn't called the last part, but I knew you were lying. I don't think you're lying now, though I so badly want you to be. Vampires have to be monsters, and you don't seem to be one. It's still possible, and if you are, I'll kill you, but I don't think you are. I don't like the implications that vampires can be that human."

"You are."

I meet her eyes, staring. "I'm a killer. There's barely anything else left of me. I hunt vampires, and that's it. I barely sleep. I don't bother eating. I just kill. So if a vampire can actually be as human as I wish you were only pretending to be, that means a lot of things that I'd rather not think about. But it also means I can't kill you, and I'd rather not let another vampire do so." This is far too much of a moral quandary for my taste. I'm so glad I get a simple villain to kill. It's far easier to work through.

"That mean I don't owe you after we kill him?"

"Oh, you'll definitely owe me."

She giggles. It seems so out of character for the big scary black-market vampire, but it's frustratingly cute. "Well, once I've paid you back, perhaps I'll manage to prove that I'm as wonderful as I implied, and I'll finally get that story from you. I don't like not knowing things, but I don't have any connections in Iraq. I only know about your time in the States."

"I don't like talking about it."

"I'm not sure you like talking in general."

"Then stop making me." I stand and straighten my jacket. "We have a vampire to kill."

Chapter Fourteen

"Y our truck is disgusting," she mutters as we get out in front of the hotel. She grabs her claymore from the meager back seat and straps it onto her back in the middle of the street. That's asking for trouble.

"You could've driven yourself."

She runs a finger along the hood, leaving a smear in the dust.

"And have you go in without me?"

I groan and slam the door. "You want to pay for a carwash, we can get one on the way back."

She shrugs. "All right."

I stare at her, blinking.

"It's, like, five bucks. Sure, we can get one. I'll even buy you food if you'd like. You're killing the man who's been stalking me my entire unlife. You think I'm worried about some chump change?"

"It's a trade. I'm doing this for you, and you're giving me the info."

"That's hardly a fair trade, now, is it?"

I narrow my eyes. "Well, I did say you had me—"

"Yes, I did love that imagery, but my point is that you're helping me with something monumental. I'm sacrificing—or at least, potentially sacrificing—a lot to help you, but I wouldn't be alive if not for you. Once we've taken care of this, I owe you quite a lot, and I'm happy to help. And from what I know, the man you're after is a monster, so I'd rather he not be free in my city in the first place. If anything, you're still doing me a favor."

I grit my teeth and check my weapons, trying not to feel sick. A monster just said I'm doing them a favor.

"God, you look like I told you I killed your cat."

"I don't like it. This was a trade to get what I needed. You're not my friend. You're—"

"A monster? A leech? What derogative do you intend to sling at me so you can insult yourself?"

I stuff my hands in my jacket pockets, burying my feelings. We need to get this over with so I don't have to be around her any longer than necessary. "Let's go. I don't know how you expect to walk right in with that thing on your back."

"It's never given me any trouble before. People don't usually stop you when you have a big-ass sword on your back. It's something you'll learn once we're friends." She smirks.

I glower at her.

"God, you can't take a joke, can you?"

I head toward the building. If I have to deal with this ridiculousness, I'd like to at least get to kill someone. "It's not that."

"Sure it isn't."

"I've told you, okay? You're a vampire, and yet if what you said is true—"

"It is. I admitted to you that I'm a liar, and you already caught me in one, but that doesn't make me a killer."

"Big talk from someone with a claymore on her back."

She chuckles. "So you can be funny."

"I wasn't joking." I glower at her. She's a vampire. She's everything I hate. And no matter how hard I try, I can't.

She steps back. "What now?"

I groan and shake my head. "It's nothing."

"No, tell me."

It would be so much easier to just kill her. Why couldn't she just be a monster? "I think you're proof that vampires don't have to be evil. And I hate that. And every second I spend with you is proving to be more unpleasant, but all that means is that we're killing *people* when we kill them. If you—and, I guess, Mia, another fucking innocent vampire—are proof that vampires are just as capable of being good, then what does it say that we're walking in to kill a whole bunch of them?" She makes it so hard to not see myself as the monster. I keep killing these things, and now I keep finding out that there's more to them than that. Am I really any better than the man who did this to me? I have to be. I can't be that far gone.

"I never said I was a good person. That was all you."

I roll my eyes and open the front door. The air is cold inside, but I can hardly feel it. Not having blood really does change how you interact with temperature. An air-conditioner hums overhead, and the scent of freshly baked cookies wafts in from a waiting area.

"I didn't think you were so much of a philosopher."

"I just angst a lot."

She laughs again, only to stop halfway and stare at me when I don't smile. "I don't understand you."

At that, I actually do smile. Why would I ever want a vampire to understand me? We walk right past the receptionist, and I revel in puzzling the vampire who's frustrating me.

She was right. The receptionist doesn't say a word as she strides in with her sword and twirly skirt. I push the button for the elevator. It opens, and there aren't vampires waiting for us. That's disappointing. I was ready for the fight to start. We climb in and hit the button for the top floor.

"Do you have a plan of any sort?" she asks.

"I was going to kill them all. Seemed a good place to start."

She glares at me.

"They're vampires. We use the hallway to funnel them. If they have guns, well, I hope I can shoot them first. If they only have melee weapons like most vampires, then we turn what would normally be an easy kill zone into a bottleneck where they can't use their numbers to their advantage, and we carve right through them. A claymore isn't exactly an ideal weapon for—"

She holds up one of the kukris the hit squad had used.

"That'll work."

"They didn't seem too attached to their toys once they were dead."

She makes it so difficult not to smile. I'm trying not to like her. She's already joking about being my friend, and I know that if I actually let her into my life, she'll try to stick around. I don't have room to care about people. The last time it happened, they all died, and all I can let myself worry about is killing the bastard who did it. There's no time and no room for anything else. But I'm almost there. I'll kill him by the end of the week, if this goes right. What do I do then?

It doesn't matter. I shouldn't expect to survive avenging myself upon a vampiric soldier who's been expecting me for over a decade. All that matters is that I take him with me. And I'd rather not have any new friends mourning me. Not her. Not Cleaver. And definitely not that stupid kid who James better have helped out. And one-hundred-percent, not in a million years, would I consider letting that demon mourn me. I'd crawl out of hell and kill him myself if he even considered pretending to care about me.

I draw my machete and magnum. From what she said, the suite isn't near the elevators, so we could risk scaring some civilians, but I'd rather be ready for whatever we find.

The first hallway doesn't have anyone, but there's definitely the stink of the undead.

Lots of them.

"I didn't think he'd still have this many," she whispers. "We should head back. We can lure them into a trap. They'll keep coming for me."

"And he can make or buy more."

"Then so can I."

I shake my head. "If it's a war of attrition, the one who's willing to feed off and turn people is going to be the one to win. Are you willing to do that?"

"No, but I don't think he is either. Would he do that when he's going to all this trouble to kill me just because he's upset that he made me?"

"People get stupid when they're obsessed. But now's the time. They're not expecting us. He thinks you'll run away again."

"Then why are there so many guards?"

She has a point there. "Then maybe they are expecting you. But not me."

She purses her lip, her brows furrowing. "So we're walking into a trap rather than being smart and trapping him?"

"Probably not."

Her eyes narrow.

"It's the best option we have. Or would you rather wait around with no idea when or how he'll attack next? I'd rather not have him blow us up while we're thinking of a better plan. I don't think we can recover from a bomb."

"He can't either. Let's blow this place up. We can pull the fire alarm first to get everyone out and—"

"Exactly my point." Goddamn it. She actually is a good person. I want to be wrong about her so badly. I want her to be another monster who I have to put up with in order to have my revenge. "We aren't willing to kill innocents to stop him. He won't worry about that. He'd blow up your warehouse with your employees inside it."

"I sent them home."

She has to be lying. No vampire is this good. "Then you can't run your business. Let's take our chances and kill him now."

"Are you sure you aren't rushing us so we can kill Reynolds?"

"Of course I am, but this is still the best option. If we wait, we have no idea what he'll do, but if we act now, we know what we're walking into."

"Fine."

Apparently, that's it. I didn't think I was that persuasive. She leads on, and the smell only grows stronger. There have to be two dozen of them. Some seem to be in the hallway around the corner, but others are through the doors on either side.

The hair on the back of my neck stands up, and I grab Dorenia and pull her to the wall as a bullet bites through the door right where we'd been standing. I had smelled one close and heard him start to squeeze the trigger, the hammer pulling back.

"You saved my life again," Dorenia says, looking far too fondly at me.

I shoot through the door, kick it off its hinges, and slice the head off the vampire crying and bleeding on the floor. "They know we're here now." At least I get some vampires to kill. I'm pretty sure they're not secretly upstanding citizens.

A door behind us bursts open, more vampires spilling past it and into the bedroom with us. It looks like only two, but they're fast. Coagulated blood sprays out as Dorenia kills hers, but mine grabs me as soon as I turn. I kick at her legs, but she moves them back. She's young, must've been barely out of her twenties when she was killed, but she looks nearly feral, her teeth chomping at me as I pull her back. Vampires shouldn't eat other vampires. It won't kill them, but if they're not full of fresh blood, it's like trying to eat spoiled food. Though, I suppose I did just eat, so I may be fresher food than I was thinking. She has my arms pinned as she wrestles with me, but it doesn't give her much leverage.

Her teeth move for my throat again and again, so I headbutt her right in the nose. She yelps, not letting go, but her grip slackens enough that I can pry my gun free and fire into her gut. My machete finishes the job. "Fuck. Okay, this might be a trap."

Dorenia scoffs. "You think?"

"I really didn't expect them to be expecting us."

"Probably as soon as his goons didn't report in, he marshaled his defenses."

Damn it. I should've thought of that. I sniff and listen. They're moving, but they don't seem to be hurrying toward us. They can smell their dead comrades, and they'd likely rather not join them. They're going to lie in wait. They know that we have to keep moving, while they have all the time in the world.

There seem to be three in the next room, a few across the hall—it's tough to tell around corners and through that many doors—and more clustered closer to the suite. How many rooms did he book? We must be killing half the hotel's clientele. "Let's head back to the hallway," I say, jerking my head toward the interior wall of the bedroom instead. If they can hear, they'll be watching the hallway, and we'll take them by surprise.

Dorenia stares for a moment before understanding dawns on her, and her lips curl into a smile, showing her fangs. Vampires should not have that cute of a smile. "Yeah, like you said, it lets us bottleneck them. We'll keep moving toward the suite and keep their numbers limited by forcing them to fight us in the narrow corridor."

"Exactly." I wish I had a way to see through walls. Thermal vision wouldn't work too well against vampires, but surely something would show them better. Maybe an X-ray?

Dorenia draws her claymore and steps in front of me, then jabs at my gun with her hand, staring pointedly. Cover her. Got it. The blade cleaves right through the wall and into the next room. The vampires on the other side make a shocked noise that I will treasure to my dying day as I charge through the opening and fire two rounds into a startled vampire. The other seems to be smarter. He rushes me and I spin, catching his blade on mine and putting a round between his eyes.

"Goddamn," I mutter. "How many are left?"

Dorenia climbs through the opening, her skirt catching and forcing her to tug it free. "Too many. I doubt we can get away with that again."

"Probably not." I pop open my gun and replace the spent rounds. Someone fires through the wall from the hallway, but the bullet flies a couple yards to my left. Nevertheless, we drop to the floor. I'd been ready to save her again, but she didn't need to be told to duck from bullets.

"I have blood with me," she says. "Worse comes to worst."

Still on the floor, I press against the wall we came through, using the meager alcove the best I can, and she does the same. Some other vampires must have liked their friends' idea as gunshot after gunshot rains over us, filling the room and keeping us from moving any closer to cover. All we can do is hope that the walls and toilet in the bathroom will slow or stop their bullets. A few even try aiming along the floor.

One clips my hand, but it looks to be a nine-millimeter, and the missing top of my middle finger doesn't overly worry me. I've had worse cuts grading papers.

Dorenia rolls her eyes and reaches for the blood, but I wave her off. "Probably gonna need it after. It's my left hand and not even a full finger. I'd rather not waste blood."

The gunfire dies down. Either they're out of bullets or they're waiting for a sign of what to shoot. I get up and kick open the door. The hallway is full of vampires. Mostly middle-aged men in suits with kukris but some younger guys and girls too with their own assortment of weapons. Is my theory that he's making them and siccing them on us correct?

Before I can act, they rush me. I get off a few shots before the first one takes a swing. I catch his sword, but someone else swings a giant axe, and I have to leap out of the way, and disengaging lets his sword take off my finger. Damn it. I need to start using something with a handguard.

I flip the machete, switching to an underhand grip. Without my index or middle finger, it's harder to guide it. I fire through the guy with the axe, and he falls to the floor as I take both hands from the swordsman.

But it's nowhere near enough. There are still four guys with kukris, another woman with a katana, and someone with a smaller axe, but the last one has an honest-to-God spear and runs at me. I try to jump to the side, but she barely has to adjust her grip, and it pierces right through my belly and into the wall behind me.

The door opens, and Dorenia's claymore takes out the nearest two—a kukri and the katana—before they can react, but the axe girl goes for her as she swaps to her kukri now that we're back in the hallway.

I slice through the spear, and the girl's eyes go wide. "Fuck you," she shouts, swinging her stick for my head.

My machete is too sharp to block wood. It'd just make the top go right on through and hit me, so I stop her in the middle of her swing by cutting her hands off, then take a deep breath and walk off the spear.

I think I scream. I'm honestly not sure. The battle is loud with the crying injured vampires and the shouts and collisions of combat. I feel for the hole in my side with my gun hand. I don't know why. I don't need to try to keep anything in, and feeling how bad it is won't help, but I shudder when I find it bigger than I expected.

I finish off the one who stabbed me just in time to fight two vampires with kukris.

"What do you think the two of you can actually accomplish?" one of them asks.

I gesture at the pile of bodies. "Quite a lot, by the looks of it."

He snarls and slashes at me, but he jumps before I can reply in kind. I raise my gun, but instead of the reassuring bang of my magnum firing, I receive a searing pain, and the edges of my vision go white. The other one took my hand off. God, I've never had the best luck with keeping my body parts when fighting vampires, but I swear it's getting worse. Maybe I shouldn't be fighting so many at once. You'd think I'd learn eventually. I'm only here for one, but I always have to get involved and make things harder for myself because I'm addicted to killing murderous monsters.

I swing for him, but it's sloppy, and he easily bats my machete away with his kukri while his friend lunges, adding another hole to my belly.

I grit my teeth. I can manage this. Dorenia has her hands full with her own assholes. I can't expect backup. The two of them close in, neither bothering to attack. They think they've won. It's one guy with slicked black hair and a kukri in his left hand on my left, and a right-handed blond on my right.

My gun is on the floor behind them, still in my hand. If I could get to it, this would go a lot smoother, but I'm not sure I want to rely on my chances of keeping my remaining hand long enough to fire with the way this fight is going.

Plus, I lost my trigger finger, and that makes firing awkward. Machete it is.

I feint for the one on the left, and he jumps back so I keep moving, swinging it to hit the other one. It's harder underhanded, but it's doable if I put my weight behind it.

The one on my right brings up his kukri to block, so I kick his leg out from under him and punch down with the machete as he drops to the floor. The other one is behind me now, and I hear his step on the soft carpet. If he's already swinging, there's no way I can turn in time. As I start to move, I hold my right stump up and catch his kukri on the bone, feeling it splinter with a grating crack. I stumble. There's not enough blood left to spray out.

He smirks and yanks his knife free, no doubt thinking he's won.

I finish him the same way I did his friend. At my worst, I can still take someone out while they're recovering their weapon.

I collapse to the floor. Blades clash against each other a few feet away. I need to help. If she dies, then I have nothing. And maybe I'd rather she be alive either way, as vile as that thought is.

Apparently, I don't need to worry about it, as by the time I finish blinking, she's standing over me, unscathed, her sword back in its sheath. "How do you always get so destroyed? I thought it must've been a one-time thing."

I try to snap at her, but I can barely manage words.

She pulls one of the blood packs from the side of her skirt and rips it open with a fang before handing it to me, licking her lips. "It's delicious. O positive."

I latch on to it, not bothering to grump that I can open it myself. She's right. It tastes amazing. She holds my hand in place while I drain the whole thing and manage to stand, the missing fingers regrowing. I holster my gun and open and close my hand, testing it. It feels as good as new. "Some of us don't have guards on our weapons."

"Then use a grown-up sword."

"Machetes are cheaper. Besides, I'm used to them."

"I'll buy you a sword. Hell, I'll buy you a dozen."

Damn, she really could make me like her. "I'll keep it in mind." I sniff. There are a few more, but they're all clustered around him in the suite. It looks like I finally get to meet the villain from her story.

CHAPTER FIFTEEN

Dorenia

She made it look so fun before. How can I resist? I kick the door to the suite open. I can smell him. He's so close, I can taste it. Two of his men rush me, but my claymore is a lot longer than their cleavers, and they don't get anywhere near before they fall to the ground. "It's been a hundred and sixty-five years," I say. "But it's time to fucking end this." At least I managed a decent entrance. That should make this feel all the more triumphant. I finally have the chance to stop him, to end him for good. I don't know what he'll try to pull, but between the two of us, we can beat him. He's fast, and he's strong, but I've had years to practice now. I can do this.

His cane sounds from the next room, and the door opens. He walks out looking as kempt and gentlemanly as ever. His suit is more modern, and his hair is shorter, but I'd know his face anywhere. "I have to say, I never thought you'd actually get this far. You've always been rather…" He taps his cane a few times, sucking on his lip. "Inept."

"Well, what can I say? I'm a slow learner, but I've had a lot of time."

"Far too much time," he spits. "You were a meal. I did not make you a vampire."

• 139 •

"Well, it didn't stop—"

Kalila raises her gun and fires.

I expect him to dodge. To pull off some mad vampire trick that you'd see in a 90's or early 2000's movie, but his brains paint the wall, and he falls, his eyes wide.

"You wanted him dead, right?" Kalila asks. "I assume the whole last conversation wasn't the important part. If it matters that much, I guess we could tie him up and give him your other blood bag."

My mouth opens, but I don't know what to say. I shake my head. I've built this moment up for so long. He's haunted me for over a century and I knew that someday, it would come to this. That I'd have to fight him again, that I'd suffer, that it would hurt, but that maybe, just maybe, I'd be able to beat him. I'd built up resources, knowledge, all to keep my family safe from him. And all it took was a bullet to the head. "No. Thank you. I've built this moment up for so long and I didn't expect it to be so…"

"Anticlimactic?"

I nod.

"You said he was fast. I didn't feel like losing my limbs again."

"No, it was smart." I stare at him, slumped and nearly lifeless on the floor, only the occasional twitch as the last vestiges of his being try to cling on. He's really gone. Or close enough. I approach his body. There's practically nothing left of his head. It's disgusting. I want to throw up. But I could nearly dance. Maybe I will tonight. It's been quite a long while since I last danced, maybe since I left my caravan, and I've well earned it. I fought my way here, and I found the only ally who's ever been able to actually make it all end. I didn't get the closure I wanted. I still don't know who he was or why he was so obsessed with fixing his mistake. But now, I can finally finish the job, thanks to Kalila. I carve off what's left of his head, making sure he won't be able to come back. "I can't believe it's over."

"Does that mean I get to have the same feeling soon?"

I nod. She's only doing this for her own cause, I know that, but it still takes me a little aback. "Yes. I will call and arrange a meeting. He's been putting out feelers for you, and the rewards have gone up since you came to town. Perhaps I can even get the money to buy you all those swords by setting this up."

"Just don't—"

"I'm not going to double-cross you."

"No." She shakes her head. "You won't."

I take a step back.

"It's not a threat." She sighs and looks around, grabbing a chair from the meager dining room table and sitting. She gestures across from her.

I stare at the body for a moment and listen for any footsteps. I smell more vampires, but no one seems to be coming, so I take the chair. "I'd say you're being all serious, but I'm not sure you're capable of anything else."

She nods, tapping her fingers on the table. "I..." She sighs, her jaw moving side to side. "I let him talk long enough to confirm your story. I trust you. I fucking hate it, but I do. You're a seedy black market information dealer, and you're quite possibly the only decent person I've met since I died."

"As you pointed out, I *am* a killer."

She nods again but doesn't raise her head, staring at the table. "Why do I want to trust you?"

"Maybe you liked that barrel idea too."

She doesn't even react. I don't like it. She's normally so abrasive. I can already barely handle her being genuine, but she's not going to at least shrug off my flirting? The heartless murderer can't be getting a crush on me, can she? What's going on? "I haven't let anyone into my life since my wife was killed. I don't bother learning people's names. I..."

"Are you asking me out?"

She manages a glare, but it's half-hearted at best. "Did you mean it when you said you were planning on being my friend?"

I chew on my lip. I said that, didn't I? Why do I feel this odd closeness to her? She is an angry, closed-off book who looks very hot in a leather jacket. Is it because she saved my life and killed the man who's been tormenting me for over a century? I suppose those are good enough reasons to fall in love with anyone—not that I'm in love with her—but I feel like she should actually have some more redeeming qualities. Though she did mention her ex-wife. I didn't know about that. Isn't gay marriage illegal in Iraq? It still is. How did she have a wife? Should I press? I hate not knowing things. But she's starting to open up, and I don't want to push her. "If you mean, was I being serious? No, I was teasing you. But you…" I point at the dead body. "If it wasn't for you, I'd be dead several times over, and you apparently have someone equally bad, who did the same to you. I want to help. Even if I didn't owe you."

"Okay." She sighs.

Did I disappoint her? Should I have added that I'd take her up on that bending-her-over-something idea? "Tell you what, once we're done with all this and we need to get out of town and lay low for a while, you can meet my family."

She tilts her head, studying me, her eyes narrowing. "You seriously keep in touch?"

I nod. "I love them. And now that he's gone, I'm rather tempted to see about going home. Or maybe moving them out here. It's a lot easier for us in Canada than it is in England."

"You don't think someone might take revenge against them for us killing him?"

"I don't know. I'll have my people look into things. Maybe we'll see once we're done. Hell, maybe you can help move them here."

Her brows furrow. Good. I don't want her being all happy at that idea. I hadn't realized what it could mean for her to meet my family. Damn, do I actually have a crush on this murderous asshole? At least she doesn't seem to be crushing on me. She's just lonely. I can be her friend. I just don't like how easy it is. "Let's go.

I have some calls to make, and I need to tell my employees they can come back to work."

She nods, looking so forlorn. And definitely not cute. I pinch the bridge of my nose. Why am I so weak to badass women in leather jackets? I'm from the 1800s; it wasn't even a trope then.

I give her a smile as we head for the door. She looks as on edge as I feel when we step into the hall, but none of the vampires attack. Maybe they know he's dead, or maybe they didn't want to help in the first place. Hell, they could even be unrelated vampires. Toronto is full of them.

"Guess we're in the clear," she says as we step into the elevator.

I half expect them all to make a run for it right then, but the elevator doors close, and we reach the lobby uninterrupted. The receptionist's eyes are somehow wider than before, and she picks up the phone as we leave. "Ask for Officer Malcolm Leopold," I say to her, grinning. "He tends to handle this stuff."

I can see how hard Kalila is fighting her smile as we leave. "God, how many people do you have on your payroll?"

"Fewer than you'd think, but enough that it starts to cut into the profits."

"How much does a corrupt cop cost these days?"

"You don't want to know." I sigh. "It's depressingly low."

"A sandwich and a doughnut?"

I chuckle. Okay, that one had to be a joke. She's smiling. I'm so glad I don't have blood in my veins as I'd absolutely be blushing. She has an amazing smile. Her eyes crinkle a little, showing actual fucking laugh lines, and that's completely ignoring the eyes themselves, which are a deep brown that make her hair look all the darker in comparison. "A hundred bucks. Not even weekly, just whenever I need something."

"You were right. I didn't want to know that."

"Like I said."

"I've been pretty broke, but I'd like to think I wouldn't cover up crimes as a cop for that little."

"You'd rather cover them up for free as a civilian?"

Her gaze hardens, but the laugh lines are still showing. "When I have to."

I grin and barely keep from asking about what she would do for a hundred dollars. Maybe it's all the blood and adrenaline pumping. That's totally a thing that happens to vampires and can distort our judgment. It's not like we don't produce our own blood or anything.

She stops in front of her truck, looking like she's seeing it for the first time. "Did you mean it about that carwash?"

I chuckle and smile at her. "Yes. I absolutely did."

Later, as we pull out of the carwash, she has the faintest smile on her face. "It's nice feeling like I actually helped someone. With vampire hunting, you're so often far too late, and any victims are long dead."

"Well, in all fairness, I am long dead."

She nods, a flicker of pain showing. She does struggle with the idea that we're vampires, doesn't she? "Back to your office?"

"I could go for some burgers and maybe some beer?"

"We have that call to make. And we don't need to eat."

"We might not need to, but it can still be nice, especially after a fight like that. And I'll make the call as soon as we get back if you want. I just need to check with some of my informants for the information, but I feel like we should probably relax first. We went through a lot."

"He's..." She looks at me. There's something like panic in her eyes. It's so strange. She taps three times on the steering wheel. "It's so close. I can finally get my revenge."

"And if you want it, you can't be sloppy. We can get food, relax for the day, and plan."

"We?"

Did I say that? Damn, I suppose I did. I sigh, clinging to the ratty seat belt. "I'm going with you. You helped me get my revenge. The least I can do is the same."

"It's my—"

"And this was mine."

She sighs, and I swear she tears up, but they seem to be gone when she turns back to the road. "Fine. If we're going to be planning, I suppose some food could be nice."

"And beer?"

She sighs, but those laugh lines show again as she pulls onto the road. "And beer."

CHAPTER SIXTEEN

"There's a shower in the office if you want to get cleaned up," Dorenia says as we walk into her warehouse, which is now suspiciously empty of bodies or any traces of blood and has a number of workers walking about, taking inventory. How did she get them here this fast?

"You have a shower in your office?"

"That's what I said."

"Why?"

She grins, and I look away. "I've been homeless too many times to not want a shower at work too. We're kind of covered in blood. I thought it might be nice."

"Now you sound like you're offering to take it with me."

"Well, if you'd prefer—"

"I don't have any clothes here. I can eat while covered in blood and get cleaned off once he's dead."

She looks so disappointed. Was that a genuine offer? Earlier, her flirting had seemed like it was simply to throw me off balance, but now that I think about it, the last few times haven't felt as insincere. "Then you do want the meeting for tonight? I thought we agreed to rest first."

"Fine. I can shower at my hotel."

"All right. I don't want you leaping into this half-cocked."

"You mean like we did with yours?"

"And look what happened to you! I keep having to save your life. I'll gladly do it again, but I don't want to have to." Is she worried about me? "You make him sound pretty scary, and so does everything I've learned about him, so please, let's be careful here. It's my life too, you know?"

Adding that it's about her life doesn't make sense. She's only helping because she wants to. She's actually worried about me. "I didn't ask you to."

She sighs and opens the door to her office. "Sure, I'm doing it willingly, but that doesn't mean it's okay to get me killed because you were feeling stupid."

"I said we'd go tomorrow. That gives us a whole day to plan."

"And I thought it was a day to relax." She looks at her clothes and her leather chair, then takes one of the seats across from it instead.

I take the other one and pop open a beer. I almost never drank back home. I sniff it and try not to wrinkle my nose, but I possess the same sense of smell as a particularly adept greyhound, and the beer smells like rancid piss.

She snorts, beer coming out of her nose. "Fuck."

I glare at her.

"Do you not drink? Wait, shit, I didn't even think. You're Muslim, aren't you?"

"Not anymore." I lean back in the chair. It's comfortable enough that I could pass out. "I kind of lost the faith after everything. I tried. It wasn't like religious stuff hurt me or anything, but how could I believe in a god that let that happen?"

She wipes her face with a napkin from the paper bag, not taking her eyes off me the entire time. She looks ready to jump out of her chair.

"You're trying so hard not to ask."

"I need to know," she whines. "That's what I do. I'm an *information* broker. And sure, imports and exports and all that, but I know things. I know everything relevant in Toronto. And there are two people in my town who were involved in a story that has them both trying to get info on the other, and I don't know what happened."

I smirk. God, she's annoying. Why is it almost adorable? "Well, the way you were laughing at me, maybe I should enjoy your suffering."

"It was a funny face."

"Sure." I roll my eyes, but I can't manage to not smile. Why is it so easy with her? Is it simply because I haven't interacted with anyone else for more than a conversation in nearly two decades? That could be it. "If I tell you, do you promise to stop bouncing like an excited puppy?"

She grabs her burger and unwraps it, grinning at me. Great, she needs a snack for this. I really am just the entertainment. "I'm not a puppy. Also, isn't that a way worse insult where you come from?"

"I've been in America for too long." I groan. "Fine. You're gonna help me kill him, so I suppose you should at least know what he did."

She bites into her burger, clearly only to force herself to be silent.

"Where do I even start? I've never told anyone before."

She swallows, having barely chewed, and can't quite meet my eyes. "You don't have to. I'm not trying to—"

"Yes, you are. You just feel a little guilty now."

"I suppose."

"There aren't too many monsters that would do that." She really is a decent person. I mean vampire. No, person.

Her lips curl, but she doesn't fully smile. It's still uncomfortably beautiful. Her features are so sharp, and it's like her smile completely transforms them, softening her. "You still don't have to."

"I'll go with when I first heard about him. I was at work, between lectures, and I called home."

"Lectures? You…" Her jaw drops. "You were a professor?"

"Of astrophysics at the University of Baghdad's College of Science for Women."

"You were a segregated university professor. And you taught astrophysics."

I take a deep breath and hold it for a few seconds before letting it out. I don't need to breathe. She's stressing me out so much that I'm breathing. "Do you *want* the story?"

"I'm just having trouble picturing it. I'd expected you to be, like, a cowboy or something. It's hard to imagine you in a tweed jacket."

"It's the same jacket, actually. It had the leather elbows, and then I had to keep replacing more and more as it tore in fights until it was all leather. Though, I suppose, it's a bit of a ship of Theseus problem as to whether it's actually the same jacket, then."

She stares at me for a long moment before breaking into a heartfelt laugh, having to wipe tears from her eyes when she calms down. "Oh my God. You were actually joking."

"I suppose I was."

"Maybe you genuinely are human."

My smile falters, and I stare at the floor. I don't deserve that. "Let's not get ahead of ourselves."

"So, okay, you called home from your job as an astrophysicist, like you're Brian May or something. What happened after that?"

"I actually met him at a conference once."

"Bullshit."

"No, I really did."

She takes another bite. "Well, I'll have to get tickets the next time Queen's touring and drag you there to prove it. But, okay, I'll shut up."

"I'm not convinced you're capable of that, but I called home. I was checking on my wife and our son. Kind of. We normally talk... talked...during lunch anyway. The invasion had been ongoing for a few weeks, and most of my classes were canceled, but not even war can stop some grad students, so we still had classes a few days a week. It wasn't like there was anyplace most of us could go to avoid it.

"She was worried. There had been a bunch of soldiers by our house. They were supposedly looking for translators, but she didn't like the way they'd looked at her. We always tried to keep under the radar, as…well." I sigh. "She was my wife. That wasn't exactly a legal thing. We claimed to be cousins, that her husband had died, and I was helping raise her child, but it wouldn't take much to see how not true it was." My hand went to my necklace, and I felt guilty for whatever flirting I'd joined in on. I'm married. How could I move past that? "I didn't take her fears seriously. I asked her to check that the oven was off. She humored me but was still going on about these soldiers. I should've taken her more seriously, but I was scared the place would burn down, and I don't know, maybe I wasn't actually as forceful about it as I remember. She didn't seem angry at me when I came home, but I swear I snapped at her about it."

"I'm sorry," she says.

Tears threaten to start falling, so I just shake my head. "When I got back, everything seemed fine. Lakia, my wife, was thrilled to see me. We had dinner. Rashad went over his lessons and told me everything he'd learned. She'd been homeschooling him since the invasion started. It was a pleasant evening. Thinking back, it always seems so foreboding. Something had to be wrong. But there was nothing. The oven was even off when I checked. I remember that fucking vividly but not the conversation earlier.

"We were watching something on TV. I can't remember what it was. Her feet were in my lap. I think I was rubbing them. Rashad was already asleep." My voice breaks. It's still so hard to go back there. You'd think seeing them in my dreams every night would make it easier.

"Kalila—"

"The door flew off its hinges. He had one of those little battering rams. He said something. God, I don't remember what. I was in shock. He was speaking Arabic, poorly, and I think he said something to the effect of us being the only people there who didn't seem to have any friends. That no one would notice if we disappeared. I think that's what it was.

"My wife tried talking to him, telling him to leave. Her English wasn't as good as mine. She said it was our home. I don't know what she was thinking. I realized he must've been one of the people looking for a translator, and I thought maybe that was what he was talking about. It didn't make sense, but I hoped it was. That he was trying to conscript us and not..."

I take a deep breath. "I said I'd do it. I could translate. I was a university professor. I knew English and could say technical stuff. He smirked at me. I thought it meant that was what he wanted. That he'd leave us alone.

"He didn't."

"I'm sorry," Dorenia whispers.

I stare at her for a moment. I'd almost forgotten she was there. "He pinned me to the bed and all but killed me, leaving me unable to even move and made me watch as he killed my wife and son. I couldn't look away."

"I'm sorry," she repeats.

I drain the beer and don't throw it up. I can barely taste it, though it still stinks. "When I woke up, I had no fucking idea what had happened except that they were dead. I tried to find him, of course I did, but I was blind with hunger. I ate one of the soldiers. I have to assume they were a friend of his. I hope." My voice cracks, and I close my eyes, forcing myself not to be back there, seeing his lifeless body beneath me. He had to be one of Reynold's men. "Maybe I simply let myself believe it. He'd shipped out. It had been his last day of service, and so the fucking bastard wanted to have some no-consequence fun. We were just the unfortunate victims. He murdered my wife and my son because he wanted something to remember Iraq by. That's what another soldier said. That he found a girl to have some fun with before he left, to remember Iraq by. I killed him, of course." At least that one I know deserved it. I unclench my hand, finding the shards of the beer bottle in it.

I brush them off and continue the story. "And knocked over his box of ammo. He must've been loading guns. I hadn't noticed. But I sure as fuck noticed then. It was all I could see. I had no idea what was going on. My OCD has always been an issue, but this was something different. I had to count every last one before I could leave. It wasn't that many. And as fast as we are, it only took a few seconds, but it was like my body was being taken over and forcing me to do something I didn't care about. Though, I suppose it was always like that with the oven too."

"Wow. I've never actually met a vampire with a counting weakness. It's common in so many myths, but I didn't think it was real."

I nod and try to take a sip, only to be reminded by a remaining shard of glass my palm that I don't have a drink anymore. I pry it free. It barely even hurts after all I've been through. "There, you have your story."

"I didn't…"

"I have to kill that fucker."

"Yes," she agrees. "We do."

"Are you sure? You know what kind of monster he is now."

She nods. "He's even worse than mine."

"I don't think I'm up for planning now. Call me when you have the meeting set up." That took more out of me than the fight, and I don't want to be anywhere near her now. This crush or whatever it is just feels wretched when my wife is still rotting in the ground, and her murderer remains freely running around town.

She reaches out as I stand. "Kalila—"

I shake my head. "No, it's okay. I just haven't had to relive that so vividly before, not while I was awake."

"I'm so sorry. You don't have to be alone."

I stare at her. "I'm not fucking you." That ruins what little interest I had.

"I didn't mean it like that."

Well, now I feel bad for assuming. "Okay, because I'm still mourning my wife."

"I mean, you look like you're not in any shape to be alone. Or to drive, for that matter. I have a guestroom at my place. You can sleep there if you want."

That's tempting. My hands are shaking. I'd rather not crash my truck. "My clothes are at my hotel."

"Then at least let me take you there."

"No…I mean, yes, sure, you can take me there, but, no, I'm not willing to cower like this. I'm not backing out of planning to murder him because I talked about what he did to me. It should only focus me. I have to make him pay."

"And we will. So let's figure it out."

"Okay. Fine. Find out where we're meeting him and get whatever plans you need for the place, and hopefully by then, I'll have stopped shaking."

She reaches for me again but seems to think better of it and only gives me a weak smile. "All right. I'll get you home and start making calls. Just, take care of yourself, okay?"

I grab my burger. "I am. See?"

That smile returns, but it doesn't seem fully real. She looks so worried. About me. That's not something I'm used to or entirely comfortable with.

She takes me home and then presumably makes her calls, and I simply have to hope that I'm not being an idiot trusting someone for the first time since I died.

CHAPTER SEVENTEEN

Someone knocks on my door. I rub my eyes, trying to wake up. The dreams were as bad as ever. I'd think after explicitly describing the story, I wouldn't still relive a version where they died from my forgetting to turn off the oven, but I suppose brains can be dumb like that.

I touch my necklace. I loved Lakia. I *love* her. I've devoted my life to avenging her, and I'm not letting some weird not-even-crush get in my head, no matter how much it gnaws at me.

I go to the door, gun in hand as I check the peephole. It's Dorenia. "Weren't you going to call?" I say as I open the door.

She stares, holding a massive bag in her right hand, and shakes her head as she walks past me and into the room. "You didn't answer your phone."

I rub my temple. Today is going to be exhausting. Wait, no, it isn't. I get to kill him. I can feel myself grinning, any sleep or traumatic dreams vanishing. "You set up the meeting?"

"Of course I did. It's for midnight tonight."

I test the weight of the gun in my hand. I need to shoot out his knees and elbows with it. I want him to suffer. "And what about the planning?"

"It's taken care of. He picked a meeting place that I'm not overly keen on, an old factory that he seems to own through a shell company, but I have the blueprints—"

"You couldn't get him to meet anywhere else?"

"Apparently, ever since a crazy vampire came to town and started killing everyone she met and asking about him, he's been rather hesitant to go places he doesn't feel safe."

I sigh. "All right. I suppose that's hard to argue against."

She smirks. "Exactly. But you'll be happy. I have presents for you."

I want to be irritated, to mock her or insist that I don't need gifts from vampires. Why can't I hate her? "What is it?"

"Well, I said I'd get you, what, ten swords? I didn't see ten that I liked, but I thought it might be nice for you to not keep losing your hands and fingers. I'm not sure I can do anything about your legs. You are so weirdly fragile for a hardened warrior." She empties the contents of the bag onto the coffee table, and I have to catch one as it falls to the floor. "What do you think?" She grins, her face softening.

I pointedly look at the weapons as they're what I'm focusing on. I'm avenging my wife. I don't need to be distracted by a pretty smile. There's a katana, a longsword, a claymore that matches hers—already trying to get me to wear a matching set with her, that's a terrible sign—a scimitar, a dao, and what looks to be a machete with a full bell guard. I pick it up, studying it. I've never seen anything like this before.

"I think that was supposed to be one of those tacti-cool weapons for, like, cosplay and such, but it's full tang, and I tested it on a few targets, and it works perfectly."

I give it a trial swing. It feels right in my hand. The balance is a little more shifted toward the hilt, but they seem to have done the best they could to compensate by adding more weight to the head. The notches and holes in the back to try to give it more of a survival knife feel don't terribly match my needs and will likely be full of viscera before the day is over, but if it means I don't have to get used to a whole new type of weapon right before the fight of my life, then it seems like a worthwhile trade. "I love it."

Her smile grows wider, and she stares at the floor. "I thought you might."

I turn it in my hand, testing it. The bell guard is a little in the way if I want to flip it to underhanded, but I only do that when I'm missing a finger, so if it stops that from happening, it's probably worth it. "Yeah, this is perfect."

She giggles, still looking away. "Good. I figure I should go in first, and then you can come in once we start talking."

"No." I run a finger along the flat of the blade. "I want to be there. I need to face him."

"You want him dead," she says. "You killed my enemy because you knew he needed to die. So does Reynolds. You won't be able to stand there without instantly starting shit. Don't be stupid."

I grit my teeth but nod. "Fine. We'll go with your plan. He just better fucking die."

"He will." She reaches for my hand but stops halfway, and her arm falls back to her side. "I promise."

"God, I want to go there now. At least I could set up, find a good vantage point to watch."

"And attract his attention."

I groan. "I know."

"Now we just have to kill time. I wonder how ever we could do that." I see her glance at my bed only to seem to stop midway. Why is she acting so nervous? I understand why I'm being weird, but what could possibly be getting to her? She's normally so flirty. Why would she start being strange about it right now? Is it because she knows about my wife, or is there something more to it? Some ulterior motive? No, I know she wouldn't. I'm just looking for reasons to vilify her.

"We're not fucking."

"I didn't…yeah, that's fine." A hint of affected disappointment shows, but if I didn't know any better, I'd think she sounded embarrassed. Maybe I'm overthinking things.

I take a seat in front of my new swords. "Let's put some coffee on and go over this plan again. I want to be ready for when we finally get to kill that motherfucker."

❖

Her villain hung out in a big fancy hotel that we spent like five minutes in, and yet mine has to pick a disgusting old factory where I have to wait for over an hour. I groan, trying to get comfortable. Dorenia insisted that I stay in the truck, but I wanted to be able to watch. Other than all the graffiti and used syringes, the second-floor control room isn't the worst place to hang out. The cameras and monitors are long destroyed, but there's a window that looks out over the factory floor where she's patiently waiting.

The old chair is barely in one piece, but it's still better than having to sit in needles and condoms.

Finally, a door opens, and footsteps sound through the building. Two pairs of them. I hadn't expected him to come alone, but this is far better than I'd feared. The door at the back of the hall opens, and they walk through. Even eighteen years later, my stomach drops when I see him, my nails digging into the chair and tearing off the armrests. He looks exactly the same, save for his hair being longer and him not wearing a uniform. He's in a T-shirt and jeans with a duffel bag slung over his shoulder. It feels so strange seeing him in normal clothes. I'd looked forward to his blood staining the camo.

With him is another man from the picture, Jacobs. He's dressed about the same and has his own bag. Did she ask for that much money? She never actually said what the deal was. I should've been more suspicious about that, but I keep stupidly trusting her for no reason.

She hasn't betrayed me yet.

"I take it you're Reynolds?" Dorenia asks. She's speaking casually, but it's easy enough to hear up here.

"And you're the information broker." He sounds so casual, so normal. He's not supposed to be a normal person—vampire. Monster. It doesn't matter how normal he sounds, there's nothing human about him. The armrests crumble in my hands. "Why the big show of it? You wouldn't tell me much on the phone."

"You wanted to find her. I can set up a meeting," Dorenia says. My eyes narrow. She knows I'm here. It's not a betrayal. She's setting him up. She has to be.

He looks her up and down exactly like he had Lakia. "And what makes you think I'd want that?"

"You want her dead. You've made that abundantly clear from everything I've heard. I assumed you'd want to do so. I can set up a meeting where you'll have the drop on her."

"Or she'll have the drop on me. Why should I assume you're not working with her?"

Shit. Of course he'd expect it, that doesn't surprise me, but what if she doesn't answer well? She could give me away even without meaning to. Dorenia brushes her hair back and chuckles lightly. "Would it make any difference if I was? You have the resources to hire me when she certainly doesn't, but if she was seeking the same thing, are you implying you couldn't take her in a fight you were both expecting?"

He spits. "The fuck did you say?"

"I know about your record. I assumed a soldier like you would be able to take care of himself. You don't need to trust me, only to know that you'll have the chance to see her, just as you want. Of course, if you don't think that it's worth the risk, I can leave, and you can be stuck trying to figure this all out yourself. I doubt you'll have anyone else offer a deal half that good."

He doesn't move, instead staring, looking ready to kill her. I should take the shot. My magnum isn't ideal at this range, but I think I could still get him. But I'd risk hitting her.

"All right. Set up the meeting."

"The money first."

He groans and pulls something from his pocket. I bring my gun up, but it's only his phone. "Fine, give me your routing number." He hands over the phone. Then what's in the bags? What does he have planned? Guns? They're not moving quite right for that. Money had made sense, but guns don't fill a bag like that; it's too uniform.

"All right, the transfer is finished. Let me make a call, and she can be here in only a few minutes."

"Then you *are* working with her?"

"You both want the same thing, I'm simply an honest woman running my business. Now may I call her now, or do you not want to meet her here?"

He snarls, showing his fangs, but she doesn't react. It's a little hot. I did not just think that. "Fine. I'll wait here."

She presses a button on her phone, and mine doesn't ring. "Hi, yeah, he'd love to meet with you. I'll send you the address." She taps something on the screen, then pockets the phone and turns back to him. "All right, it should only be a few minutes. She's not far."

"Because you told her where we were meeting?"

"Not until now. I simply told her to be nearby."

"And you think she wouldn't figure it out? Have you checked that she's not tracking you?"

She steps toward him and juts her finger at his throat. "And you think she's not tracking you? You're the one she's looking for."

"Yeah well…she didn't know where I was."

"Except that you were looking for her. It wouldn't be hard for her to have taken the same role I did. How do you know she wasn't any of the people calling to inform on her? You've had, what, I'd guess a dozen informants?"

"Not quite."

She shrugs. "I'm just saying, I'd recommend checking that none of them were her. Though, I suppose you're about to kill her, so it'll hardly matter. Were you going to wait in here? It seems like it'd be a hard spot for an ambush."

"She's right," he mutters, jerking his shoulder toward the door, the bag shaking. "We'll set up in the hallway."

I don't need to be told twice.

They'll hear me, of course, but I can beat them there.

I run as fast as I can and don't even hear any footsteps until I hit the stairwell. "Shit!" someone cries.

As I kick the door open, I find them looking around the foyer. They haven't had time to ready for a fight.

My shiny new machete is dirtied with the fresh blood from his friend's neck. "Fuck!" Reynolds shouts, trying to pry an assault rifle out from the duffel bag. So they were holding guns, but there's something more in it, a big cloth bag. I don't have time to look any closer as I slice through the hand on his weapon.

He screams. It's the most wonderful sound I've ever heard. Reynolds's suffering. They should bottle this. As I swing again, he jerks the bag in the way, and my machete slices right through it, only for rice to spill all over the floor.

No.

No.

No.

I grip my weapon, trying to swing it, but my eyes keep watching the rice spill out. I can't ignore it. It's overwhelming.

He dumps the bag on the ground, but I can only tell because more rice spills out as I hear him running away. This is so stupid. Another set of footsteps follow him, and I can smell Dorenia, but I'm not even up to a thousand.

One thousand two hundred.

There's so many of them. I need to go.

But I have to keep counting.

I go through every single fucking grain of rice while my only chance at vengeance gets away, and there's only one way he could have known.

CHAPTER EIGHTEEN

Dorenia

Fuck! I breathe in, closing my eyes, trying to track him. His blood stops a little past the door. There must not be much in him, but I should still be able to smell him. Even with a car, it shouldn't have faded this fast, but I've done a circuit of the whole area for blocks and haven't caught anything other than pot and maple syrup, but it's Toronto, so that doesn't tell me much.

He must've had his car loaded with stuff to cover his scent in case he had to get away. I'd respect the plan if it didn't mean that I had to watch a murderous bastard with a missing limb get away without consequence yet again. I promised I'd help her take him down. She did it for me.

And all I did was let him get away.

I head back into the factory to find her still counting the rice with his severed hand and her hat at her feet. He planned out everything. Except, perhaps, for losing quite so much. I thought I'd set it up well enough, but the bastard is more paranoid than I feared. I should've known that. He's been here for years, and I know almost nothing about him; that should've told me so much. How did I miss everything?

"He got away," I whisper.

For a long moment, she doesn't say anything, but she finally mutters, "499,763." She's shaking as she turns to me. Her teeth show, and her eyes are narrowed. "I had him. He was right here. I got his little fucking friend, and he got away. Because he knew."

I take a step back. She's still gripping her machete, and combined with how angry she looks, it probably isn't a great idea to be a vampire near her. "We'll get him. He had his car loaded with strong smells that are all native to the area, so it's hard to track him, but I know I can find him again. It shouldn't take long. A few more days and we'll kill him."

"He knew," she snarls. "How did he know?"

"How did he know to bring rice? That's what you're asking? I don't know. Is there anyone who—"

"You are the only person I've ever told. The one person in the past eighteen years that I've trusted. You talked to him without me there and set up this meeting. He knew. You're the only one who could have told him."

"I didn't!"

She steps toward me. "Then how the hell do you explain this? He should be dead. There is no reason he is still alive except that someone told him how to stop me. You are the only one it could be."

I stomp closer, glaring up into her eyes. Of course she suspects me. I can feel anger rising up but not like it should. I want to feel betrayed that she blames me, but I get it. "I didn't! I would never."

She looks away, but the fire in those eyes doesn't go out. If she doesn't kill him soon, she's going to kill someone else. "Is there anyone who could've seen?" I ask. "Who else have you gone to in town?"

"No one. I haven't told—"

"But they could've seen something."

She shakes her head, but when she speaks, she doesn't sound as convinced. "No."

"Who?"

She sighs, crossing her arms, the machete pressing against her shoulder. "I've gone to a few bars, talked to a couple other vampires, I went to the Community Center, met that demon and that other information broker. No, I didn't do anything that would give it away. It has to be you."

I'm so glad she doesn't sound convinced. I reach for her and hesitate but rest my fingers on her shoulder, just above the blade. "I swear to you, Kalila. I didn't betray you. I..." What? Am I going to confess my feelings? I don't even know what they are. It's a crush, and saying that I wouldn't betray her because I have a crush on her is the most childish thing I've ever heard. "I know too well what it's like. I have been in your sexy combat boots, and I would never put someone in that position. You know I don't need the money, and you know how much I owe you. I swear that I didn't tell him."

She sighs.

"I didn't."

"Then who did?" She pulls away but sheathes the weapon. She believes me. I force myself not to smile. It would look awful given everything that's happened, but it means a lot that she didn't immediately murder me. "It doesn't make any sense."

"You saw Vincent? That's who you mean by information broker, right?"

She nods.

I stare at the ground. How would he know? "Did he knock over anything in front of you?"

"No, he..." Her eyes widen. "Yes. But it was only some pens, and I picked them up. He wouldn't...it didn't...How would he know to do that? It doesn't prove anything."

"It's not proof, no, but it's evidence. Please, tell me that's enough to at least entertain the idea that it wasn't me."

She sighs. "I'm already entertaining the idea. I want to believe you, it's just—"

"I get it. It looked bad for me, but it's starting to be a bit better, right?"

She nods.

"Okay. Then I'm going to send some of my people to start finding Reynolds again while I have a few words with my competition. Taking him out will only benefit me, so trust me, I have no qualms with handing him over to you."

"Good."

Why? Why does she do it for me? I've spent my whole life cowering from a murderous vampire; how does another one make it sexy? "I assume you still have some anger you might want to work out?"

She quirks an eyebrow. "What did you have in mind?"

I chuckle. "Nothing scandalous." Does she look disappointed, or is that simply my wishful thinking? "I know a group of vampires in town that have been getting out of hand. Hunting people, attracting attention. They're all babies, even younger than you, but they don't respect how things are done in Toronto."

"I don't respect how things are done in Toronto."

I roll my eyes. "Yes, and you've already gotten banned from the Community Center for your trouble. Maybe you can start earning your way back in by taking care of the worse troublemakers, but regardless, I know you want to kill. Do you want me to tell you where to find them, or should I leave you stewing until I find Reynolds and wring a confession out of Vincent, since you can't go see him anymore?"

Her jaw clenches. "I do need to break in my new machete some more."

"That's what I thought." I send her a quick text. "All right, that's the address, so you can have your fun while I take care of things. I promise, I—"

"I know." She finally meets my eyes, and my heart breaks. She still looks betrayed, as if she can barely face me. She's on the verge of tears just looking at me. It's so not her. I have to look away. "I believe you. I hate that I do. I shouldn't trust you. I thought I'd finally been proven wrong, but...If you were lying, then you're going about it in an incredibly strange way. I may be an idiot for it, but I have faith in you, Dorenia. I'm sorry for faltering there. I should've known better."

"No." I step toward her and freeze, realizing exactly what I was thinking of doing. I'd even started reaching for her cheek. I jump back, letting out a nervous chuckle. "I get it. It's fine. You didn't...there was no reason...you had every right to think it was me, given the available evidence. The fact that I'm still alive and in one piece says a lot."

"I'm sorry."

I shake my head, staring very determinedly at the floor rather than facing her and risking seeing if she realizes that I'd been about to kiss her. "I get it. You go kill things, and I'll do my job." I grin, my laugh sounding less awkward. "Honestly, you're doing me a favor. Being the only information broker in a city this size, God, I'll have no end of customers."

"Thank you." She leans in to eye level, but I still can't face her. "I know I'm a difficult person to work with."

"It's nothing."

She pulls her phone out and stares at it. "How many are there?"

"Should be four."

She sighs. "God, that's barely a workout. Oh well, at least I'll feel a bit better. It just has to be his throat next time."

"It will be. We'll kill him. You won't be haunted by him anymore."

"I'm not so foolish as to think it'll make him go away. I just don't want him to be able to enjoy it."

I finally look at her, but she's still staring at her phone. I'm not sure if I'm relieved or disappointed. "Killing my tormenter seriously helped me. It might do more for you than—"

"I'll always blame myself." She turns to me, and those beautiful eyes still look forlorn. If she wasn't about to kill someone, she'd probably be collapsing in tears. "But it doesn't mean I won't obtain a certain satisfaction from him meeting his fate. Call me when you find him or when I get to kill Vincent. I shouldn't be more than an hour. They're only twenty minutes away."

Don't say it's a date. "I'll let you know. Until then?" I step closer and realize yet again that I'm thinking of kissing her. Okay, maybe a crush is underestimating it. I wish I could understand why. Trying to cover it, I pick up her Stetson from the ground and hand it to her.

"I'll see you then." For the slightest second, she leans in. She corrects it immediately and snatches the hat from my hands, but I know my senses are too keen to have misread that. She wanted to kiss me.

The door slams behind her, and I can't stop grinning. Good God, a few minutes ago, she was barely keeping from killing me. I was terrified of her. There's no reason I should already feel like this.

I bite my lip, knowing that I'd be blushing if I could. It's not just in my head. This connection really goes both ways.

I shake my head. There's no time for this schoolgirl nonsense. I call up Howard, one of my oldest employees. "I need you to look into someone. Gregory Reynolds, his file should be on my desk. I have a recent address, military records, transaction history. Find out where he'll be before he gets there or at least where he'll stay long enough for me to meet him."

"Of course. It shouldn't take long."

"It will. He's slippery. He has twenty shell accounts and uses cash for everything. I'm not giving you an easy job, but I need you to do it. Put as many people on it as you require. You can all have overtime."

His voice perks up. "I will! Why is this so urgent?"

Because I'm putting pleasure before business and trying to make things up with a girl I like? "I owe someone a favor, and I don't like letting those sorts of things go unpaid."

"I understand. I'll let you know the second I know anything."

"I know you will." I hang up and groan as I realize we both took my car. Did I give her the keys?

To my surprise, my Mercedes is still waiting in the lot. Did she run? I suppose I can hardly blame her. She is trying to work off steam. A run will probably do her some good, and it's not any slower than a car anyway.

Not bothering to learn from her example, I climb in and head for the Community Center. Vincent is not likely to enjoy our little chat, but at least I know he won't try anything stupid there.

Chapter Nineteen

Dorenia

The Community Center doesn't look any more imposing than usual. It's still only a run-down old building that smells of hundreds of fiends. Nor does it feel any different when I step inside and am surrounded by them, all running about and doing their shopping, socializing, and work.

I'm breaking the spirit of the rules, even if I'm going to try very hard to avoid breaking the letter of them. Shouldn't it feel different coming here? It's been so long since I've been run out of town. I desperately hope that I don't have to go through it again.

But I'm not willing to let someone get away with hurting Kalila. If it was another client, maybe I'd have done the same, I truly don't know. It's two murderous vampires both out for blood. Maybe it's sensible to pit them against each other and go for the highest bidder, but I'm well past the point where I can look at it so objectively.

Reynolds is a monster, and my city deserves to be free of him.

And more than that, Kalila deserves to not have him haunting her anymore.

When do I ever walk into something like this without a plan? She's making me stupid. But what other option do I have? He has the same resources I do, if perhaps a bit lacking in comparison. If

I start looking into anything to make a plan, Vincent will know. So what option does that leave me?

Just one. I can do exactly what Kalila would do: march in there and give him a piece of my mind. Well, not exactly; it would be a piece of his mind on the wall if I was following her example a bit closer. But the general gist of her method is there, and perhaps it will feel good to go back to handling things the way I tried so many years ago.

I walk straight for the store, not bothering to feign interest in any of the stalls. My claymore is on my back, but it won't make me any more threatening. No one else would be stupid enough to attack someone in the Community Center, and he'll know that. I probably should've left it in the car, but I feel more confident with it.

I draw up short, staring at the open shutters of his store. What will stop him from simply staying here so long as I'm looking for him? I'm letting my anger and infatuation take me too far. Kalila's blunt approach may be useful, but it won't extract him. I have to think. I have to be myself.

How do I do this? He'll know that I'm working with her. Or at least, I would. He does often fail to live up to expectations, but I'd hate for underestimating him to be my downfall, so I should act as if he has all of the knowledge that I have.

Which means he knows I was talking to Reynolds. He has every reason to think I'm playing both sides. I can use that. Perhaps that will be enough to get him out of here long enough to confess and be eviscerated.

"Good evening, Vincent," I say as coolly as I can manage as I walk into the run-down old shop.

He stares at me with an unreadable expression while standing behind the counter. Great, I suppose I shouldn't have expected him to give anything away for free. "Not often I see you in here, Dorenia."

"Well, it seems we have a common client, so I thought it'd be useful to work together to ensure a better payday."

His eyes narrow. "Do we now? And when have you ever wanted to work with me?"

He has a point. I never went so far as to run him out of business, but there's a reason he has a shitty little shop in the Community Center, and I have a thriving business and international clients. I force a smile. "Well, if you'd prefer, I could take it all for myself as usual. I simply thought that if we pooled our resources, we could make more, but I see that I was naive. Tell me, does that faun bakery still have those delicious scones? Oh, I suppose I'll find out for myself." I turn on my heel and head back out the way I came.

"Wait," he calls. I smirk. I knew he was too desperate to let me leave without making a deal.

I turn, slowly, fixing him with a nonchalant look. "Yes? Have you changed your mind?"

He grumbles, gnashing his teeth. Sometimes, it feels so good to win these petty battles. "Yes. Fine. What did you have in mind?"

"Well, I know you're working with Gregory Reynolds and that the very vampire he's hunting has already paid you a visit."

"And who's hunting him."

Is he testing me? It's not like him to volunteer information for free, even if it's something he'd expect me to know. "Well, of course. I've already arranged a meeting for them, but let's just say, it went poorly. She went in swinging and nearly killed him, but they both got away relatively unscathed."

"And you're worried they'll blame you?"

"Oh, naturally not. They have little reason to. I'm not the one who gave away the information that actually caused the issue."

His eyes widen, but they shrink back immediately. Fair ones are always so good at keeping their poker face, so to lose it for a whole millisecond, he must be utterly terrified. Of Kalila or Reynolds?

"Yeah, Reynolds called me up after, out for blood," I say, watching his eyes widen again. He is terrified. "I had it all set up, but someone had given him some bad intel. He said he'd call me again after he took care of them. Whatever they said, he dumped rice on the ground for some reason, and she chopped his hand off."

"She...but...he..."

Oh good, I was hoping it'd be this easy. I widen my eyes, staring at him, letting my jaw drop the barest bit. "No, you don't mean...you thought that old wives' tale was real? Vincent, I'm a vampire. I've never met a single one of us who actually had to count anything that was dropped."

"No! I knocked over some pens when she was here, and she picked them all up."

"So she was polite? That was your proof?"

He gnashes his teeth, staring at the cup of pens on his desk. "No! No, of course not. I'd heard rumors."

"Ah, I'm sorry, rumors and basic manners, a far more compelling argument."

"There was nothing polite about her," he snaps. "No, I know I was right. I had to be. I talked to a vampire who said he got away from her after he spilled some corn."

"Well, then, clearly, it's the rice that was the issue. But tell me, what happened to that vampire?"

He crosses his arms, still glaring at the pens. "I don't know. I didn't hear from him again. It was years ago, and I only thought it was curious that there was a fiend hunting fiends. I didn't know the value of the information, so I didn't put enough effort into it."

"Maybe she let him get away so he could lead her to others. Did he have any companions?"

He sighs, screwing his eyes shut. "Yes, I believe he did."

"Well, then, it seems you're the one Reynolds intends to kill. I suppose I should leave before he gets here."

"What? No," he shouts, moving closer to me but still behind the counter. "Please. You don't think he'd actually kill someone in the Community Center, do you?"

"Tell me, did he seem more in control than his target? She killed someone here just the other day. It seems they're two peas in a pod." The comparison makes me feel sick. Kalila has plenty of problems as a person, but she's not like Reynolds any more than I'm like my own nemesis. We're the monsters they made us, but we're a far cry from the monsters they are. "I should hurry. I'd really rather not get dragged in—"

"Please," he cries. "Please, help me."

I wonder, can I both lead him to his death and profit from it? If I'm going to get rid of the competition, I may as well get paid. "What's in it for me? You're asking me to betray the confidence of a client and put myself at risk for what I could charitably call my biggest competitor."

"Anything! Please. I'll leave town forever."

"And you'll also do that if he kills you."

He closes his eyes. I can see this pains him. I try not to enjoy it too much, at least on the outside. "I'll give you my clients. And the intel I have on them. Obviously, I can only give you what I've written down, but it's more than you'll get if Reynolds has the chance to trash my store." A big assumption, but I don't bother to question the leap. "Please. I need the money to get out of town, but I can give you everything else."

"All your clients and intel?"

"Written intel."

"Does that include everything on your computers?"

He chuckles. "Computers? I hardly touch the things. But, yes, I have a computer back there." He gestures toward the rear of the store. "It's by my bed. It doesn't have much, but I tried updating my notes on there, and I have some research I've done."

How old is he to be so behind the times? I'll admit, I thought they were nothing more than a fad back in the 80s and 90s, but eventually I had to accept that they were the way of the future, and I like to think I've learned them quite well. "All right. Grab the notes and computer and let's get out of here."

He scrambles over the counter and starts shoving things into a bag. I stand by and watch. How long will Reynolds take to get here if he's really coming? How many notes can I justify leaving behind? I suppose I can always get them later. "Shit, is that him?" I shout.

Vincent screams, dropping some of the notes. He falls to the floor, picking them up and looking around.

"We'll head out the back." I grab his elbow and drag him out of the store. The rear exit to the mall is heavily boarded up, but every now and then, someone has to make a daring escape, so there's just enough give in each door to allow us to slip by and manage to squeeze into the alley and go around to my car.

By the time I unlock it, Vincent is hyperventilating. "It's all right," I say. "We're almost there."

"Where are we going?"

"I know someone who can help you get out of town. It might take some of that money you squirreled away, but it should be easy enough. You can hide out in my office until I arrange the meeting."

"Thank you," he screams, wrapping his arms around me. "Thank you so much."

I smile as I pat his back. "It's nothing. Come on, before he tries looking outside for us." He climbs into the car, and we head right back to my warehouse.

"Your guy can really get me out of town?"

"It shouldn't be an issue." I lead him up the stairs to my office, open the door, and let him through. Then I slam it behind us as Kalila stands from the couch, still covered in dried blood.

Can I trust her to play along? I suppose it doesn't matter that much at this point. Vincent doesn't even seem to be looking at me. He's quaking in his loafers as she approaches, machete in hand. "So is it true? You saw me pick up your pens and decided to tell Reynolds rather than giving me any useful intel?"

He shakes even more. "I—"

"Tell me," she snarls.

"Yes! I thought that you had a counting weakness. I'd heard of it before, and it seemed justified. Another vampire had mentioned it years ago. I knew it had to be real. I had no idea it was an affectation."

She stares at me.

"I told him Reynolds is coming for him because he was wrong about your weakness."

She smirks. Goddamn it. There should not be fluttering in my belly from how sexy she looks when she's about to kill someone. "Oh, she must have misspoken. *I'm* coming for you."

He quivers. "It was nothing personal."

Fluorescent blood spatters my office and my favorite skirt. He keeps screaming for a while too, but eventually, she figures out something that'll even kill a fair one, and the noise finally stops. At least I had some good beer to drink while I waited.

CHAPTER TWENTY

I'm sorry," I say, not quite willing to meet Dorenia's eyes. She's sitting on the couch, as far from the mess as she can get. I'm sure I'm covered in what could vaguely be called blood, but she deserves to hear the apology. Though, I suppose I could always use her shower and say it again.

"For covering my office in fae blood? Goddamn, you got it everywhere."

"I'll clean it up."

"You'd better."

With a heavy sigh, I force myself to meet her eyes. To my shock, she doesn't look horrified, angry, disgusted, or any of the rational reactions she should have to my killing someone for having betrayed me. I wouldn't call it loving, exactly, though I'm not sure if that's because I don't want it to be or because it actually isn't, but she looks caring. "I will, but that wasn't what I was apologizing for."

Her eyes narrow. "Then what?"

"For doubting you. I assumed that you had to be the one who did it, and I should've known better."

"You've told literally one person in your entire life what your weakness is, and the next day, someone else knew. Rather than immediately killing me, you actually heard me out and listened to my side. I appreciate that you feel bad about it, but believe me, I completely get it."

"I still should've—"

She stands and is suddenly far too close to me. Her hand clutches mine, and if I needed to breathe, I'd probably faint, as I don't think I can remember how. Her lips are way too close, and I hate how much of me wants to close that gap. "It's okay. If I'd been in that same situation, I would've been just as convinced. And lest we forget, I did tell you my weakness the other day, so you could've easily done it. And you could've assumed that was a trick to get you comfortable enough to reveal yours. You had so many reasons to suspect me, and instead, you let me find the person who actually did it and did the whole town a favor by taking out those vampires. I trust that went well?"

I nod. "I caught them feeding. Some poor girl. She got away, though I suspect she'll be quite traumatized."

She gulps, one of her fangs digging into her lower lip as she gazes at me.

I take a step back and clear my throat. "Did your people figure out where Reynolds is?"

"Why, so you can kill the sexual tension by avenging your wife?"

She does love putting it all right out in the open, doesn't she? "I wasn't…there isn't—"

"So you're saying that if you didn't feel obligated to your wife, you *still* wouldn't be pushing me against this wall and having your way with me?" She gestures to the side.

I stare at her for a long while. What can I even say? I'd use the couch? I'm not that much of a top? It doesn't matter how badly part of me seems to want this. I can't. I'm married. I still owe that to her.

But what about once she's avenged? Can I justify moving on then? My hand flies to my necklace. It's still there, as cold, metallic, and unalive as ever. It's not her. She's been gone for eighteen years. What is it that's still keeping me from moving on? Is it only the need to kill the bastard who took her from me? That I'm afraid that if I move on, it'll kill that need in me? "The only thing that's kept me going for so long has been a need for revenge. If I…Sorry, no. I can't believe I'm even saying that. So, yes, you've found him?"

She stares at me, responses seeming to war behind her eyes. I just said something incredibly dumb, and there must be so much she could reply with, but maybe she sees how much it hurt. She takes a seat behind her desk and flips open a folder. "Yes. He has a manor a little ways out of town. I have the address here. It's, apparently, a rather swanky party destination for some of the elite in Toronto. It's still in his grandfather's name, and I haven't ever put the two together, and I'm incredibly disappointed in myself for it. I hadn't expected a vampire like that to be, well, a rich playboy. He's a soldier, but apparently, he inherited some money right before he was recalled, and he fled the country. The estate was in legal limbo, so he was able to take the manor without actually taking ownership of it. I should've caught it. I had his accounts and everything, but none of that included anything this big…" She groans, staring at the papers. "He had a good accountant, and I don't like that I let it slip past me, but yes, I know where he is. Or at least, where he should be. No one has a place this hidden from prying eyes and then doesn't stay there when they piss off their worst enemy."

"Enemy makes us sound on equal terms. He's a pest, a leech, and I'm his exterminator."

"Poetic," she mutters. Is she angry at herself for missing this or at me for rebuffing her?

"Dorenia…" I bite down the words. What am I thinking?

She shrugs. "I'd advise we go in the morning. From everything I've seen on him, while I don't think he's particularly weak to the sun, he may be more bothered by it than you or I, so it's likely to be the best time to get him."

"You still want to go with me?"

Dorenia scoffs and shakes her head. "How many times do I need to say it?"

"I just thought—"

"That you were too hot and cold toward me for me to still want to kill a murderous asshole who's stinking up my city? No, I'm good with this."

"Okay...Maybe once he's gone...No, one thing at a time."

She laughs. Why? Why the hell is she laughing? I thought she was mad, and I didn't say anything funny. "You're really struggling with this. It's kind of adorable. Was she your first love?"

Tears well in my eyes, and I don't want to risk saying anything. I nod.

"I'm sorry. I promise, we'll avenge her. Maybe it'll help."

I nod again.

"Clean up all this blood and then go take a shower. I'm going to order takeout. Chinese and O positive sound good?"

"Is the blood Chinese or—"

"I don't have a way to specify that, and it's never seemed to affect the taste. I was thinking egg rolls and some orange chicken with brown rice."

I actually laugh. "Sure, I could eat."

"Now that's a surprise."

I roll my eyes. "I eat at least every week or so."

"Sure you do."

I shake my head. "Where are your cleaning supplies?"

She points toward the door. "Closet a few doors down. If you reach the next hallway, you've gone too far."

It doesn't take long to find, but the blood certainly takes a while to clean up. By the time I finish my shower, the food is starting to get cold.

Dorenia looks up at me, chow mein slithering between her lips as they turn up into an unashamed smile. It's so weird having someone actually happy to see me. Generally, they're more pleading for their lives. I wish that I couldn't feel myself smiling back at her all the same. It feels like I'm betraying Lakia. I know she's gone. I know she's not coming back. But she's all I've been holding on to for so long, and letting myself be human again and actually feel something feels like I'm dishonoring her memory.

Though, I suppose she'd disagree. We never actually talked about what we would do if one of us died, but I'd like to think I knew her well enough to know that she wouldn't want me spending the centuries moping and becoming more of a heartless, murderous monster.

But how can I know I'm not just using that as an excuse?

I sit opposite Dorenia and look over the food before helping myself. "Do you really eat food every day?" I ask, taking a bite of lukewarm chicken.

She nods, wiping sauce from her chin with a napkin. "Always have."

"Why? It seems like a waste of money."

She snatches an eggroll from the box and bites into it. "Why wouldn't I? It's part of being alive. And it tastes good. We're not monks. When I was a human, I didn't live off nothing but plain bread if I could avoid it, and I don't see any reason to do the same now. The whole ascetic spartan thing sort of works for you, but it can't be healthy. I know you love, well, enjoy the misery of thinking of yourself as a monster, and while I'm sure there's some comfort in pretending that's all there is to you, you're still a person too."

I rip open a soy sauce packet with my fang and dump it onto my plate. "I'm starting to see that."

"Better late than never."

"Hey, we haven't all had over a century to get used to what we've been turned into."

She gasps, her smile only growing as she holds a hand to her chest. "Bringing up my age on the second date. I should walk right out."

I cough, choking. I can feel the chicken lodged in my throat, but without the need to breathe it's more a discomfort than panic inducing. I hit my chest hard enough that I can feel my ribs strain and manage to actually swallow my food without having the most embarrassing vampire death imaginable.

"Did you just almost die because I said it was a date?"

I cough. "Um…"

She rolls her eyes. "God, you're fucking terrifying in a fight, but you genuinely have completely forgotten how to be a person, haven't you?"

"You don't have to be so blunt about it," I mutter.

"Coming from the person who shot my nemesis in the middle of a conversation, I'm not sure you have any room to complain about bluntness."

"I was simply being practical."

She crosses her arms, that smile never disappearing. God, I hate how beautiful she is. I could sharpen my machete on those cheekbones. And there's something so inviting about her expression. Maybe that's why I keep barely being able to stop myself from kissing her. The way her eyes linger on mine, her smile so full and content each time she sees me. It's overwhelming.

"I should go home," I say.

She stares at me.

I stare at my plate, squeezing my index finger in my other hand. "It… I… We should be fully rested before we go to face him in the morning."

"And what if he knows where you're staying?"

Shit. That's actually a good argument. "He could know I'm here?" I try, not sounding at all convinced of it.

"He may well, but I suspect my office, or even my condo, is more secure than the motel you're staying at."

My mouth goes dry. "I'm not…"

"Oh my God." She chuckles, and even when she's laughing *at* me, it melts my heart. "Are you worried that I'm going to seduce you if I take you home?"

I tap my chopsticks on the plate, not able to bring myself to face her. "I'm worried that you won't need to. That if I keep spending time with you, that, well, maybe something to the effect of that shoving you against the wall idea you suggested. Or, hell, maybe you'd do it to me. And, no, I'm not trying to give you ideas. I don't know why I seem so incapable of resisting you. I haven't liked anyone else, fuck, ever. Not really. It was always her, and when she ran off to Najaf, it broke my heart. You don't need my whole sob story—"

"I don't mind hearing it. Maybe it's just my need to know things, but I want to know more about you."

I groan and grab the water bottle she set out for me, unscrewing the cap as I try to sort out what to say. "She got a job there, and we stayed in touch, but it seemed like nothing was going to happen between us. We'd been best friends since we were kids, and I'd told her how I felt ages earlier, but she had either been too scared or actually hadn't returned my feelings at the time. She told me later that she'd been too scared, but I don't really know. A year later, she came back. She'd lost the job, and she was pregnant. I offered to help, and it all escalated from there. It was always her for me, so losing her, well, it broke me."

"Why do I suspect that part of you doesn't want to risk the chance that you might be able to be put back together?"

"Because you know me too well for someone I've known for two days?"

She swigs her beer. "I thought that might be it."

"My rage is all that's kept me going for so long." I screw my eyes shut, fighting back the tears. "I can't lose it. And I can't attempt to move on before that bastard is dead."

"I get it."

I finally meet her eyes, willing myself not to look angry but not to look too loving either. She looks away, so I'm not sure what it ended up being. "Do you? Few enough people can understand what it's like to have someone do that to you, to violate you so completely and turn you into this thing, and you get that, but you've never had your wife and son stripped away from you in the process. I'm not denying your pain, and I do appreciate that you're one of the only people in the world who can relate. But even you don't really know how it feels."

"I suppose not. He took people from me, but it was over years and years. I never lost everyone at once, and I managed to keep most of my family alive. So you're right, I don't completely understand, but I'm willing to try."

I take another bite of chicken. It does taste good. Maybe I should try eating more. "I don't think I can be done processing it or be in any place where I can try to move past it while he's still alive. And I know that if I keep staying so close to you, I'm going to end up doing something before I'm ready."

"Now that I do understand." She reaches for my hand but must realize the irony of grabbing it right then as she instead picks up her chopsticks and helps herself to more noodles. "He'll die tomorrow. Then, maybe we can have a proper date. But until then, you can sleep on the couch in my office. My condo is nearby, so I'll be here in the morning to get you, and we can go kill the asshole keeping me from having a hot girlfriend. Okay, that was tasteless. I'm sorry."

I snort. "No, it's fine. I have a bad habit of raising the tension. You don't deserve that. It's nice to have it broken."

She rises and walks around the desk, far too close to me, but she keeps going until she's near the door. "There's some blood in the mini fridge, and beer, but I assume you won't want that." She giggles. "Try to sleep. You'll need it. I'll be here bright and early. I have absolutely no idea what to expect." She sounds pained as she says it. "I've gone through all of his accounts, and he shouldn't have security, but I know there were at least a few guards at one of the parties I was able to find photos of. I don't like it. But I know that you'd never stomach spending a few days doing recon."

"It would give him time to prepare. I'm not allowing that."

"He's had years." She sighs. "But I said we'd go in tomorrow. And right now, he's scared. Maybe it's the best time to strike, no matter how much I hate it. Or maybe I'm simply looking for excuses to help you hurry up and process, and I'm being completely selfish. I hope not, but it's a chance. So if we die, I'm haunting you."

"I look forward to it."

Her smile grows again as she studies her feet. "Well, sweet dreams." She closes the door behind her and leaves me to finish the food and try to get comfortable on the couch. I should've asked for a blanket, but I suppose I've slept in worse.

I can't stop thinking about the morning. About killing him. About what it could mean with her. But mostly the killing.

At some point, the planning and fantasizing turn into dreams, and both the revenge and the consummation grow substantially more graphic. It is a massive improvement over my perpetual dream of losing everyone I love in a fire caused by my leaving the oven on.

Chapter Twenty-one

The door opens, and I grab the machete from under the couch, already on my feet.

"Good morning, then," Dorenia says, grinning at me from the doorway.

I turn and pick up the sheath, returning the blade to it. "Knock next time."

"It's my office."

"And it would've been your neck this went through."

She sighs, but I can still hear the mirth in her voice as she says, "You're not a morning person. I'm starting to see that. Would you like some coffee in your blood?"

"I don't need blood," I mutter.

"You don't want to be at your peak when you fight him? I guarantee he's drunk up, probably enough to have a new hand."

I groan. "Fine. Blood and coffee, then, but I'll take it to go. We need to leave."

She sets a couple cups of coffee on the table. "Drink enough that I can put the blood in if that's what you want. It'll keep it warm. I might do the same for mine. That sounds delicious now that I think about it."

I drain half the coffee. It doesn't do much for me anymore, but I suppose the pantomime of humanity has its own uses.

She tears open a blood bag and pours it into both of our cups. "I assume you're going to insist we take your truck?"

"I had to go for a run the last time we took yours."

"And I suppose I don't terribly want mine destroyed. Fine, we can take your old beater, but if it breaks down on the side of the road, that's on you."

"It won't. I've had it for years, and it hasn't failed me yet. At least, not more than a few minor issues, like struggling to start up or the lights or AC acting up, but we hardly need those."

"You're filling me with confidence."

I roll my eyes and throw on my jacket and hat. "I'm ready." I take a sip of the coffee. "Damn, that is good."

"French press from a local shop. You might've noticed if you weren't inhaling it earlier."

I take a more appreciative sip before giving a dramatized contented sigh. "Happy?"

"You're driving, come on." She claps her hands.

I fish my keys out of my pocket, and we head to the parking lot to find my truck patiently waiting to aid in exacting my revenge. Damn, I'm actually in a good mood. I'm not used to this. I can feel myself grinning as I start the engine and pull onto the road, following the directions on her phone. "It's really happening."

She gives my bicep a reassuring squeeze and based on the way she's biting her lip in my peripheral vision, enjoys it far too much. "Yeah. It won't be much longer."

"He's had it coming for so long."

"We're immortal, so I'm not sure that I'd call eighteen years so long, but—"

I glare at her.

"Okay, I see your point. It's been far too long." She glances toward the back seat, where her claymore and the shotgun she brought from home should still be sitting. "I've never actually used this thing in a fight. I bought it for home defense. With incendiary rounds because it's home defense from fiends, but it's never come up."

"It'll be fine," I say. My own weapons are pressing against me under my jacket. Anyone sane would put them in the back or the seat while they drive, but I get too much comfort from knowing I'll have them if anything happens.

Such as if the same car has been behind me for a solid five minutes, not taking any of the chances to pass, and taking the same turns. I take a loop that's out of the way but will still get us to Reynolds.

The car keeps tailing us the whole way.

"I have to admire your restraint for not simply shooting out their tires the second you suspected they were following us. You have grown as a person."

I roll my eyes. "I'm only like that with monsters. For all I know, this could be a cop who...Fuck." I recognize the beige SUV. I should've placed it earlier, but I'd only seen it once before.

"What?"

"I know who it is." I wait until we're on a country road with no other cars around for miles and pull to the side, putting the truck in park.

"Who is it? What are you doing? Are we going to fight him here?"

"I hope not. Stay in the truck unless you have to. I'd like to get out of this without any bloodshed."

"What have you done with the sexy murderous girl I've been flirting with?"

I close the door and stand next to it as the other car pulls to a stop a few meters away.

Cleaver doesn't shoot me. I'm not actually sure he has a gun, but he could've slammed his car into me if he was actually planning to kill me. He climbs out and stares, not seeming to want to get any closer. "I've heard some things about you," he shouts.

"I can hear you. You don't need to yell."

His expression grows even more dour. "So, what, you have vampiric hearing?"

"You're not that far away."

He crosses his arms. He doesn't have his weapon out. He doesn't want to turn this into a fight any more than I do, does he? That should be comforting, but I fear that it's going to happen whether we want it or not. "So you're saying it's not true? You're denying, yet again, that you're actually a vampire?"

I sigh.

"That's not a denial."

"I really am a vampire hunter."

"That's not what I'm hearing." His voice is increasingly gravelly, like he wants to sound intimidating to the monster he's going to have to fight. The one who betrayed his trust. "You were at that place. Their fucking monster black market. Charlie told me."

Charlie? Is that the kid? He's alive? "Did he also tell you I saved his life while I was there?"

"He said you were a monster. One of them. That you walked in just like any of those freaks. You were even palling around with a demon."

"I was looking for information. And I killed the one running the slave market and had half my bones broken for the trouble. I'm not the bad guy here."

"Then who is? 'Cause I don't know shit about you. I've fought you, I've met you twice, and I don't even know your name. And now I'm being told that you're a vampire trying to kill some ex-soldier. And Charlie didn't say anything about you saving him. He said that demon bought him and let him go."

"The demon I was palling around with. So wouldn't that suggest—"

"Shut up!" He clutches his head. I know the pain of cognitive dissonance too well not to recognize it on someone else. "Vampires don't help people. They don't rescue kids. And neither do demons. I don't know what the fuck you're up to, but you're still a monster who's come into my town and started causing trouble."

I take a step toward him, and he grabs his cleaver from his pocket holster. I stop mid-step. "I'm causing trouble for monsters. Not for people."

"You broke into someone's house."

Fuck. "They're a blood seller." I should sound more confident. They are. I'm not even sure they're human, but I see how bad this all looks for me.

"Right."

"Look, fine, I lied. I'm a vampire. That soldier asshole, he turned me into one after he murdered my wife and son. Yeah, I'm gay. Big surprise, I know. My name's Kalila. I swear, I'm not your enemy."

"And why the fuck should I believe you?"

I draw my machete slowly and set it in the back of my truck, do the same with my gun, and take a step away from them. "I've fought you before. If I wanted you dead, I'd have tried to kill you instead of just defending myself. I'm sorry, believe me, I know how much it hurts to think that there might be monsters that aren't evil. Maybe I am, if that helps, but they aren't all. I don't know what that makes people like us."

"I'm not evil. And you're not a person."

"Okay." I nod, holding up my empty hands. "I'm just saying, it's more complicated than either of us would like it to be."

"How did that soldier turn you?"

"He's a vampire."

"Bullshit. I met him. He wasn't—"

"How did you test?"

He looks at the sun, then back at me, looking mildly perplexed, as I'm not a pile of ash. "I used a cross."

"It wouldn't work on me either."

He pulls one from around his neck and holds it out.

I look right at it. It's a little sterling silver one, looks like he probably got it for about ten bucks at a pharmacy or gas station, as the chain is more brown than silver. "Yeah, that doesn't do anything."

"I've had it work on quite a few vampires."

"If you want consistency, we're a bad lot for it." God, including myself as a vampire still hurts. I've spent so long denying it.

"So what? That doesn't prove anything. You're the one who's been lying to me. You were probably at that hospital getting blood for yourself, and then you went to the market to buy some human to feed on. And some weapons. I see that shiny new machete. It doesn't look much like your old one."

I have been drinking blood. I did buy weapons there. Maybe I deserve this. "I only want to get revenge against the man who did this to me. If you want to kill me after, we can fight. But please, stay out of my way until then. Reynolds is a monster."

"He says you're one."

"And what, you trust him because you both served?" I try not to put any bile on the word, but it's hard when even the soldiers who weren't literal monsters were bombing my home.

"I didn't. My son did."

Shit. I know how dangerous misplaced parental feelings can be. They'll get all your bones broken when you're surrounded by monsters and can't keep from rescuing a child in danger. "Reynolds went AWOL. He was recalled to fight back in my home country again, to kill more people who look like me, and he ran. Does that affect your respect for him?"

"It might if I believed you."

"I can get proof." Hopefully. I doubt Dorenia brought everything with her. She could probably have it emailed to her, right? "I need to talk to the other person in my truck. I'm not going to get a weapon. I'm not going to pull anything."

He sheathes his cleaver. "Fine."

I open the door and lean in to see a rather annoyed-looking Dorenia. "Wow, you really do treat humans differently."

I shrug.

She hands me her phone. "I have his records right here. Don't break it."

"Thank you," I mouth, taking it and closing the door. "It's on this phone," I say, a bit louder. "Can I bring it over to you?"

He grunts but adds a more definitive "Fine."

I show him the open file and make sure he knows how to scroll through it, taking a moment to indicate the picture that's clearly Reynolds, from which he hasn't aged at all. How old is he? Part of me worries he might be the very grandfather he inherited his manor from. I always assumed he was turned on tour; it explained why he went on the run when he got back, but he literally hasn't aged since the picture.

"This doesn't prove anything," he mutters, but I can hear the doubt in his voice.

"It proves he's lying about a few things." It feels so strange trying to convince someone of the truth. I always rely on lies, and I certainly never let myself get close enough to worry for anyone's safety, and yet I'm baring it all to keep from having to murder him and his friends. I'm growing soft.

He grumbles. "Well, but...You're still a monster."

"I am. And believe me, I hate myself plenty for it. But he's the one who made me." That seems how it always goes. Monsters make more monsters. I hope I've never created anything like this. If any of the vampires I killed weren't the monsters I thought they were, I could've made someone even worse than me. Worse than him. "Not all monsters are the same. You don't have to believe that, but it's true. And he's a far worse one."

He bares his teeth and seems ready to throw the phone, but he must think better of it as it stays in his hand, and he stares at it. "Goddamn it."

"I know."

"I can't...you're still...God!"

I grab the phone gently and ease it out of his hand. She'd be so pissed if I let him break it.

"I don't know what to do."

I nod, trying to look understanding. I get it in a way few others could. "I'm sorry. Being a vampire hunter is complicated, especially when you're like me. I didn't want to cause problems."

He nods.

"So I can go?"

"I still don't know that he's—"

"Come on, you do."

He sighs, grinding his heel in the dirt. "I'm not helping you."

"You don't have to."

"Fine. He wanted us to take care of you. The rest of the gang is waiting up ahead. I'll call them off."

"Thank you."

He stares at my truck, squinting. "Who do you have with you?"

"A far better person than me."

"A vampire?"

I shouldn't give her away. It'd be so easy to lie, but I've done enough of it. "Yes. We killed the vampire who turned her the other day. And now she wants to help me get revenge against mine."

"I should kill you both. You're monsters. You're vampires."

He wouldn't be able to. Even with the rest of his team, they wouldn't stand a chance. "I'd rather you not."

He sighs. "It's Chuck."

"Chuck? Oh." I blink. He gave me his name? That's weird. I thought he was going to sit it out and let the monsters destroy each other. Is he actually starting to trust me? "It's nice to meet you."

"Yeah, well, I don't think I can pronounce your name. So I'm not going to try. I'll…" He opens his car door. "I'll leave you to it. Maybe I'll treat you to a drink sometime, but that's it. I can accept that you're a vampire hunter. That makes you one of the good guys. But you're still a monster."

"Okay."

He nods gravely and drives off, kicking up dirt on my favorite jacket.

As I brush it off, I walk back to my truck, hoping that meant more than it probably did. That if a vampire hunter like him can start trusting me, I'm not completely beyond redemption. Maybe I could have an actual life after all this is over. But I don't let myself actually believe it.

"That went well," Dorenia says when I climb in.

"A lot better than I thought."

"It's almost like you're not a horrible monster and shouldn't expect everyone to treat you like it."

I shrug. Maybe she's right. But for what I'm about to do, I need to still be that monster. I want to rip him to pieces.

CHAPTER TWENTY-TWO

As we pull into the driveway to the manor, lights shine out from every window. I knew he'd be expecting us, but I didn't think he'd be so blatant about it. "Maybe you should wait in the truck," I say as I pull to a stop halfway up the drive.

Dorenia glares at me, crossing her arms.

"I don't..." God, how can I say this in a way that doesn't lay everything on the table again? I suppose I can't. "I don't want him to take another person from me. I know it's new. We barely know each other, but I can't pretend I don't care about you. I can't let him hurt you."

She sighs, a corner of her mouth twitching in a half-smile. "And you think I want to let you go get murdered? You can't even keep your legs attached."

"I can!"

"Sure. You'll need me bailing you out with a bag of blood before long, and I'd rather actually be there and not be stuck out here worrying that you're already dead."

Great. This is what happens when I start caring about people. They start wanting me to not throw my life away. And that's about all I've been doing for so long that I'm not sure I know how to live any other way. "Fine. Just don't get yourself killed."

"I have over a century on you. Believe me, I know how to stay alive."

I nod. I can't imagine lasting that long. No part of me thought I'd survive today. I'm going to kill him. I never cared to walk away from this alive. And unfortunately, now I'll hurt someone if I don't. That will take some getting used to. I have no idea what's going to happen between Dorenia and me, but I might just try to stay alive long enough to find out.

I check the blade of my machete and the cylinder of my magnum. They're all as pristine and ready as I left them when I went to bed last night. They'll take his head, just as they were always meant to.

Once her claymore is restored to its rightful place on her back and her shotgun slung over her shoulder, we take the path to the front door and the short flight of stairs inset from the porch. No one shoots us. I don't even hear any movement.

There's a smell, but it's not people. I can't quite place it. Something warm and strange.

The front door is a double oak set and looks incredibly ostentatious. It's so hard to imagine him living here. "This is really Reynolds's place?"

"I suppose it could all be a misdirection. It would be an effective one."

I nod and grip the doorknob. It's locked, which is far from surprising, but it's only an ordinary door, and the lock snaps off when I pull it, the door swinging with it.

Flames bellow out toward us.

We dive to the side before I can see what's attacking us.

I didn't smell anyone. A vampire with a flamethrower seems dangerous and impractical. I normally go for a beheading, but burning will kill us perfectly well. Assuming that it is a vampire with a flamethrower, as mad as that sounds, I think I can at least figure out how to handle it. We'd have to act fast if we don't want to get roasted, as that'd actually kill us. I've seen that trick of shooting a flamethrower's tank and causing it to explode in so many movies, but I'm not sure if it would actually work. You normally need a spark, and that's hard to guarantee. So we'd have to rely on Dorenia's incendiary rounds.

I scramble to my feet, satisfied that we now have a plan. Strangely, I still don't smell another vampire. Farther in the house, maybe, but not close to us. I only smell burning and some animal scent.

Dorenia is standing opposite me, well out of sight of the door. She looks shocked. She won't take her eyes off the entryway.

Did she see something I didn't? I take a tentative step, trying to catch a glimpse. I see the open door, flames licking up its surface and already starting to burn it away. And past that, I see scales.

I squint, stepping closer. "Oh."

A massive reptile crouches on all fours in the entry hall of the mansion, its leathery wings stretching past where I can see, great claws on the end of huge, red, scaled legs digging into the tile floor.

I let out a breath, stepping back around the corner before it can decide to burn me alive. "Reynolds has a fucking dragon."

"How the fuck did I not hear any word of a dragon in Toronto?" Dorenia finally says. "What connections does he have that I've been missing? I don't fucking get it."

That hardly seems the most pressing concern. "More importantly, how are we going to get past it? What kills a dragon?"

"I've never seen a dragon before, but to my knowledge, they're killed like most creatures. You pierce their heart, brain, maybe a vital organ. The issue is the thick scales, massive size, and you know, teeth, claws, and flames."

"So I see." I sink to the ground, leaning against the porch. I could probably put a bullet in its eye. It could pierce its brain, but that could also piss it off a hell of a lot, and it has two eyes, so blinding it isn't a good bet. "Who the fuck has a dragon?"

She shakes her head, peering around the corner and promptly ducking back. No flames follow her. Is the dragon waiting for us to come to it?

"How smart are these things?"

"I don't know," she says quickly. "I really don't know much about dragons. Something that I am now greatly regretting."

"You want to reconsider that staying-in-the-car idea?"

Dorenia fixes me with another glare.

"Fine. Fine." I hold my hands up, the machete and magnum clasped in them. "So, what, do we rush it?"

"We could try going around. Maybe we can slip past it."

"Ah yes, one of those guard dragons that you can simply avoid."

"It's possible."

I sigh, craning my neck to try to see it but not wanting to actually pop my head out. "If we go to where we can't see it, then we risk it getting the drop on us."

"Or we risk surviving."

I scratch my cheek with the hand holding my gun. Neither solution seems compelling. "We could try going around the compound, but I don't like the idea of not going straight through and killing the bastard."

"Well, if you're concerned about leaving our backs exposed, then I think making sure there's no one around to sneak up on us is a good idea."

"We'd smell them," I say, breathing in deeply. It's just the dragon. That's the only scent I'm getting. Deep in the house, there's the faint scent of vampires, like a sweet, preserved corpse, but I'm not a hundred-percent certain that's not simply the lingering odor from one living here. "God, what if this is just a trap? Maybe he left the dragon here to wait for us while he escapes."

"We won't know until we check."

Damn it. "Fine, let's look around, but I'm pretty certain we're going to have to fight this thing."

She nods, and we go in opposite directions, looping around the building until we can meet at the back. The grass is well-maintained and a luscious green. There's a gazebo and a basketball court near the back, but there's no sign of any other guards. Maybe the dragon ate them. Hell, maybe it's not even his dragon, and it killed him and his retinue and stole the house. We don't know enough to have any actual conclusions.

It better not have stolen my kill.

I tighten my grip on my machete and groan. A vampire steps around the corner, and I swing. "Fuck," I mutter, stopping in midair before I take off Dorenia's head.

She brings her claymore up a second too late. "Feeling jumpy?"

"Sorry." I drop my arm to my side, not wanting to sheathe the weapon this close to a dragon.

She rolls her eyes. "I take it you found nothing as well?"

"Unless you wanted a quick game of basketball to warm up."

"I think I'll pass."

Nothing has attacked us. The dragon didn't even act except when we opened the door. I guess that means it's not hungry. I peer through a window and see an unoccupied kitchen with pots and pans hanging from hooks over a stove. I knock the window out with my elbow and clear out the glass. Leather jackets are so useful sometimes.

We climb in, looking around, weapons at the ready. Nothing comes for us.

The scent of vampires is slightly stronger. The strange warm animal scent of a dragon is unpleasantly also stronger.

Dorenia checks the fridge. "Blood. In Tupperware. That's an interesting sign."

"Were you hoping to find something specific, or were you just hungry?"

"I was curious." She pulls out a Tupperware full of thick red liquid and pulls off the lid. The scent hits me in much the same way as roast lamb, freshly pulled out of the oven, did when I was alive. My mouth waters, and my stomach aches for a taste. "God, that's fresh. Well, that's a good sign. It means he's likely here. And must've had a human around to drain. There are quite a few in the fridge, as well as a wagyu tenderloin, which just seems excessive, but I would guess it's for one of his parties. I wonder if that means he's still planning on holding them. It would be a lot easier to sneak in during a party than when he has a dragon guarding the place."

"We're already here, and he's terrified. If he hasn't already, he'll run when he knows we survived his traps, so we need to kill him quickly." I lick my lips, staring at the blood.

She pops the lid back on it and tosses it in the fridge hard enough that it opens and spills, but she slams the door. "I don't trust anything in this house. Especially with what these parties are supposed to be like. The blood is probably drugged."

I nod, forcing my gaze away from the fridge and to the kitchen door. I pull it open and step out into the hall. The scent only grows stronger.

"I think I understand now," I say, trying to focus on anything but the blood. The vague scent of vampire is lingering by the dragon, and there's only one reason he would have the dragon inside instead of waiting for us in the yard.

"What?"

I sigh. "The dragon's blocking the stairs to the cellar."

"Fuck, that makes sense."

We search the rest of the house that we can reach without getting closer to the dragon, but there's no sign of any way up or down. The scent of the vampires isn't growing closer either. It's hard to identify, but I'm confident he's hiding beneath us. It's the only thing that makes sense.

That, or it's all a trick, and he's long gone. I'd give it about fifty-fifty, but I've always been a gambler. Even if I can't cheat this time.

"I think he's still here," Dorenia says. "His scent doesn't smell strong, but that probably means he's in some sort of panic room or maybe a deep sub-basement."

"The fucker trained a dragon to watch over his panic room." I grit my teeth. "Great."

She shrugs. "So we kill it. We're vampires." I only slightly wince at the admission. "The whole issue with their scales is that they're too thick for humans to cut, but that doesn't apply to us. We cut through bone like it's nothing, I can't imagine the scales will be that much tougher."

I nod, not feeling at all convinced.

"Let's see what we can do." She holds her claymore out in a combat stance, as if she could block flames with it, and we head toward the scent. There's another door in the way, but I remember exactly what happened the last time we opened one of those around this thing, so I shoot out both of the hinges, and it sags to the ground.

A footstep shakes the floor as the dragon turns. I can see it plainly. I've left us in a kill zone. His flames can easily fill the hallway. I grab Dorenia's wrist and dive through the wall to a study. It's only plywood and insulation. Fiberglass cuts me but not enough to draw blood, and we end up on the other side a good deal dustier for our trouble while fire engulfs where we'd come from, the wall smoking.

"That's why it didn't go outside." She groans. "Not only is it a guard dog, but it's staying where it's easiest to roast us."

I shoot out the next door and reach for her hand.

"It's okay. I'll follow you. I'd rather not be dragged through fiberglass again," she says.

So I go through the wall again; this one should lead closer to the dragon, and I just have to hope that the stupid flames won't engulf me in the process.

Dorenia bumps into me as I come to a stop against a stairwell. Fire erupts in the room we'd been in. I can see it pouring out, nearly blinding in its brightness, the center a cool blue against the raging inferno of the orange and red around it.

There's only one thing we can do. We've closed the distance so much already. I charge the stupid beast.

It's bigger than I'd assumed. It looked giant before, but I'd underestimated the size of the entry hall. The stairs are big enough to walk three abreast without issue, though they only go up, but the dragon is much larger than them. He—and I can say that rather comfortably at this distance—takes up half the width of the room and would probably take up a good quarter of a football field, and his wings scrape the ceiling.

A chain collar clings to his throat, but there's no leash keeping him in place. The links are straining and red from the heat of his neck. This seems like the absolute worst thing to fight as a vampire.

He turns to face me, bringing up a foot as big as I am, with claws longer than my machete, and swings right for my throat. I drop into a slide and slash at the palm of his foot, but his skin sparks as the blade connects. Definitely harder than bone.

I leap to my feet and dash around him. I'm faster, and this thing seems to only move at about the speed I'd expect of a giant lizard, but it's so big and solid that I'm not sure there's much I can do about it.

I swing into the underside of its belly only for the blade to barely dig in. I see Dorenia avoid another belch of flames.

I yank my machete free, and the creature cries out, flames pouring out to accompany the sound. Not so much as a drop of blood comes with my weapon, and the blade chipped and twisted, but at least I know it's possible to scratch. I press my gun to the slight chip in its armor and fire a round.

It screams, so I fire again only for a foot to smash down on my back, claws digging in.

The talons are sharp. One sinks into my arm, and the nerves explode in pain, then suddenly go silent. I'm not sure if my arm is gone or simply dead, but the crushing weight on my spine and the talon digging into my shoulder distract too much to probe for an answer.

The weight diminishes.

Or maybe my spine is broken, and that changes how things feel? It's one of the only bones I've never broken.

I try to roll, but the foot is still on me. That means I can still feel it at least. I press against the ground with the hand I can still use and push as hard as I can until I manage to shove the foot off me and roll onto my back. My feet seem okay, so I jump to them. My right arm dangles uselessly, but it's still attached, though my machete is at my feet. I guess I couldn't hold on to it.

I look around to see Dorenia panting, holding her claymore and coated with a thick layer of green blood.

I stare at her. She managed to cut it. To kill it?

A basso roar sounds above me, and I look up to find the three still-attached feet as the irate dragon coats the ceiling in flames. He seems to have wedged his head into the second floor and must be panic burning. The smell of smoke is already growing overwhelming.

"How did you manage it?" I ask, trying to move my arm and failing. Great, so I should count it out for the fight.

"Speed," she says simply. "I ran around it and used all of that momentum to slice right through the leg on you. I should've gone for the neck."

"Getting sentimental in your old age?" I smirk.

She shakes her head and stares at the creature above us. "I'm not sure it's going to come back down."

"Well, we have to do something before the whole place goes up in flames. We can't find him if we're on fire." I shoot into its belly, steadying my shots, trying to make sure that I hit the same point each time. The first shot ricochets, but the second buries itself deep, as demonstrated by the green blood trickling down and the flaming roar above us. The third must've gone wide though, as I don't get any more blood, only a lot more screaming as smoke grays out the room around us.

"It's a trapped animal," Dorenia says. "I think all we can do is put it out of its misery."

"I'm trying," I snap back.

She yanks the blood bags free from her skirt and holds them out to me. I stare at them in confusion before holstering my gun and taking them as best I can. "I'm going to need one of these. Maybe most of them," she says.

"What are you doing?"

"Did you see a shower when we were searching? That'd help."

"This is stupid. You're not running through the fire to kill it. You'll die. I can just keep shooting it."

It screams, more blood pouring down as the roar of fire above us grows deafening. "I'm not letting it suffer like that. So, bathroom?"

I point to the side. "I think it was over there. But wait." I drop the blood on the floor, careful not to let them burst, and shrug out of my jacket, then have to peel it off my bloody arm and wrap it around her. "It might help."

She grins at me, leans in, and gently presses her lips to my cheek. "I hope this works. I'd rather not die trying to prevent a murderous madman's house from burning down. Even if it is also to keep something from suffering unnecessarily."

"I can—"

"You can't even swing your machete right now. You need to heal. And we're wasting time."

She takes off at full speed, and I hear a shower running a second later as she must be drenching herself and my nice jacket. I drop to my ass and bite into one of the bags, drinking the best I can. I don't want to waste any more than I have to. She's going to need a lot. We might have to use that suspicious shit in the fridge.

Maybe I should go down and try to find Reynolds while she does this, since it's not like the fire will be out, but I can't leave her to have to heal on her own. So I wait.

It should only be a few seconds, and I need to know that she's okay. Great, I really do care about this fucking vampire.

The creature shakes, not even managing a whine, and more blood pools on the floor.

Then a charred woman drops to the floor right in the middle of the green puddle. She's not in as bad a shape as I'd expected, but she's definitely burnt. I rip off my shirt and use it to smother the flames, then pick her up and carry her outside. Once I've managed to dump the rest of the open pack of blood down her throat, she manages to speak.

"I'm fine." She coughs, sounding not at all fine.

I hand her another bag.

She nods, her lips curling into a pained smile. God, I love her smile. "Go kill the bastard."

CHAPTER TWENTY-THREE

The building is on fire, and a dead dragon is dangling from the second story, threatening to drop to the floor beneath it and crush it. I should probably hurry.

I pick up my machete and check the doors until I find a set of stairs leading down and leap over nearly the whole flight, reaching the bottom a second later. The smell of smoke and flames is so strong, I can barely detect anything else, but I know he's here. The stink of the undead hangs in the air, taunting me.

"Come out, you bastard!" I shout.

No answer comes. I run down the halls. There's a storage room; some dungeon full of sex toys and whips; a vault of weapons, jewelry, and solid gold bars; and finally, tucked away in a room near the back, there's a solid metal slab of a door.

It reeks of him.

"Reynolds," I call. "I'm here."

The door looks to be even sturdier than the dragon. I knock and get a solid thud. Then knock twice more for good measure. There's no answer from the other side. Maybe he killed himself in fear. I'd hardly blame him. It would be a far nicer death than I'll give him.

I grip the door and pull, feeling it strain. My muscles ache at the effort, and I have to dig my feet into the ground and grit my teeth, but I keep pulling.

The door doesn't want to give.

It's keeping me from my revenge while fire rages through the building, already licking at my back. If I stay here, I'll burn alive, and that won't get me my vengeance either.

But how can I just leave? He's right here. I can't let him get away again. He was right in front of me, I took his fucking hand, and he still got away because of his stupid fucking trick. The bastard killed Lakia. He killed my baby boy. And he's mere feet from me.

I dig my feet into the ground, the leather of my boots melting into my skin as I pull, my nails tearing in the door.

And it still won't move.

I can turn around. I can go back to Dorenia, and we can fight him another day. If we can find him. I could live a normal life. There's something there between us, and I can find out what it is rather than dying in this fire in a futile attempt to get my revenge. He'd leave me alone. He's not hunting me down like her enemy was. I could forget it and leave with her.

But how can I go back to her like this? I don't know if these feelings are real, but I can't explore them until I've avenged my wife. I need to know that Lakia can rest easy. That this monster can't destroy another family, can't create another monster.

I look around to see if there's anything I can use to pry it open, but there's nothing; it's all already burning up, except what I brought. I take a deep breath and grip the door with one hand, trying to pull it just the slightest bit loose, then shove my machete in the barest opening. I pull, trying to lever it open only for the hilt to snap off in my hand, leaving the blade in place.

I grip the door again, prying with both hands. It's still more open than it had been, and the flames are near-overwhelming, melting hinges as surely as they're roasting me. They must have done their part, as with one last heave, it finally comes open.

I can barely even feel my flesh searing. Bloodlust will do wonders for a person. Or a monster.

And I find a monster waiting for me.

Still looking exactly the same, that pathetic excuse for a soldier is shivering in his recliner, his eyes bulging at the sight of me. A gunshot echoes in the tiny metal box, and something bites into my belly, but I cross to him and crush the gun in my hand, leaning in until my eyes are level with his. "It's over, Reynolds."

He tries to punch me, and his arm flies off, fresh blood coating the wall.

I grip the hand holding the crushed gun and yank off that arm too. He screams.

I stare down at him, pathetic bloody mess that he is.

He leaps up from the chair as if running into the fire will spare him any pain. He's actually trying to run. This keeps getting better and better. I grab him by his shoulder, blood spraying against my hand as my nails dig in.

Reynolds kicks back at me, his movement flailing and desperate, but I toss him back into the chair, towering over him. I finally get to see it in his eyes. This is it. This is how I felt. Terrified and powerless.

"You're still nothing," he snaps, but the words seem hollow, so coated in fear that they're not even an insult. "You're nothing but that scared girl, desperate to escape me. And that's all you'll ever be."

Maybe killing him is too quick. I grip his leg and rip it off, relishing his pained scream. "No, Reynolds. I'm not powerless anymore. I'm sure you remember. You gave this to me. You turned me into the very monster that will end you."

His eyes dart around the room. I'm not sure if he's looking for something to use against me with his only remaining limb or if he's hoping he can buy time until the fire consumes us both. "You turned me into this. You took everything from me. I only wish there was enough that mattered to you that I could return the favor."

"You killed my son!" he shouts.

He's buying time. It's the only explanation. But what the hell is he talking about? I stare at him. "No, you killed mine."

He snarls, tears falling from his eyes. "Jacobs. My squadmate. I made him. Decades ago. And you killed Rogers. My whole squad." He almost sounds like he cared about them. "I'd been going to turn him, but then—"

"Oh." I grin. "Good."

He gapes at me. "Good?"

My smile only grows. "Yes. I was worried there was nothing I could take from you. But look, I killed your family, your dragon, ripped you apart, and burnt your house down. Finally, you can know what it's like, what you put me through. Maybe now you'll understand why every waking moment of the last eighteen years has been spent hunting you down and why you're going to die."

He shakes, baring his fangs. "You'll pay for it. I'll make sure of it. You won't—"

He never finishes that threat. I want him to suffer more, but I can't wait. He needs to die. I try to leave his headless body behind, but fire has completely filled the basement, licking at the stone walls, and I can barely ignore the pain as it eats at me. There aren't any windows down here that I can see through the smoke. I might be trapped.

I toss his head out of the panic room and close the metal door. It swings right back open. "Shit," I mutter. There's only one thing I can do. It's going to hurt. I grab the handle of the door, slam it shut again, and hold it in place. It's solid metal. The whole room is. I can take the pain, but it's going to be like being in an oven.

I might not make it out of this. I'm honestly not sure.

But I know that Dorenia will never forgive me if I die here, so, I suppose I'll have to hold on.

I stay there, clutching the handle, holding the door closed as the flames fill the basement. The heat washes over me. I close my eyes and grip tighter, my skin blistering and going numb, but I keep holding on.

I never wanted to walk away from this. I would've been fine going out in a literal blaze of glory with my revenge. But she just had to have that smile.

So I take the pain and stand there, feeling everything burn up around me, enduring the agony of it because I have to live. I have to see that smile again.

CHAPTER TWENTY-FOUR

Dorenia

As the sirens grow closer, I can see the lights flashing through the trees. That is way faster than expected. Normally, I'd go out to meet them, but I'm currently still covered in blood and down to only a charred and bloody shirt.

I suppose I could actually use my vampiric abilities. I don't like doing it. It's violating a human's free will, and it bothers me, but assuming we're able to rescue that idiot before she burns to death, I'd rather she not be arrested for murder, and it's probably a good idea to not have a bunch of firemen discover a dragon corpse.

I hope I can do it. Shit, I've only intentionally enthralled people a couple times in my entire life.

I groan. I hate doing this.

I shake my head. No. It's the only option. Anything else will alert a lot of people to fiends being real, let people see me half-naked, and completely screw over Kalila. I can do this.

Plastering a smile on my face, I stride to the front of the manor where the fire engines are already parking, along with a few cop cars. This better work. At least they're not likely to arrest me for public indecency outside of a housefire, but I'd still rather not take my chances.

"Is this your house, ma'am?" one of them asks as he steps out, politely averting his gaze.

Should I do this one at a time? Can I even do a whole group? Probably easier this way, even though she doesn't have time to waste. "Yes, it is, and there's no one in it." I put the compulsion into my voice, hoping desperately that I'm doing it right. I haven't done it since the forties when someone tried to arrest me. "Quickly, please, put out the fire. You don't need to worry about finding anyone."

He nods and doesn't react to how weird that must've sounded. It probably worked, then. I go around, telling the rest of them the same. One of the cops comes to talk to me. "We have some clothes in the trunk," she says.

"Sure, give those to me, and then leave."

She stares at me for a moment but slowly nods. "Yes, ma'am. Right away."

I hope she doesn't have a partner. I don't see one. I throw on the sweats and baggy Toronto PD T-shirt and watch as she drives away, the firemen already spraying the house. I can't make it to her yet. I hate this. I ran through fire mere minutes ago. I should be willing to do it for her. But I don't have another way to heal, and if I can't bring her blood, then I need to be able to get her out. I can't sacrifice my life if it won't save hers. That's not brave, it's stupid.

So I wait. And I watch. Knowing that every minute she could be burning up until there's nothing left of her. She may already be long gone, and I could be waiting for nothing.

But it's all I can do. I have to hope that she's still in there, and knowing her, likely not in one piece, but she has to be save-able.

I can't stomach the idea that she isn't. That miserable, murderous, vampire hating asshole has really grown on me. If she's dead, I can't try to take her out for dinner.

The second the fire has died down enough, I run inside. Smoke and steam still billow out, filling the room. I'd be roasting if I was human, but temperature doesn't hit like it used to. As long as it's not enough to cook my skin off, the discomfort doesn't matter.

None of them follow me. I suspect that my insistence that there is no one inside must count for me as well.

The second floor is gone, with only a slight skeleton of a structure to suggest it was ever there. The dragon's corpse, however, is untouched, beyond the missing foot and head. The fire didn't do a thing to it. I suppose I should've expected that.

The kitchen is in surprisingly solid shape. The fridge is scorched, and nothing likely works anymore, but it's still mostly where it was, although if it's now charred to a crisp. I open the fridge only for the door to fall apart in my hand. The blood is still there. It's boiling to the touch, but I can stomach that.

I clutch one of the containers and run, trying to find the stairs down. I know they're here somewhere. She didn't just run into the fire and die.

The door is gone, and half the steps are burnt away, but there's still something. It turns halfway down, so I can't skip the whole thing, but I leap to the landing. It gives way under my feet, but I kick off it and land at the bottom of the steps.

The basement floor is in better condition. It's cement, and the walls seem to only be scorched. I touch one, and it doesn't fall apart.

A door crumbles as I pass it, and fire still smolders inside, but there's nothing suggesting a person there. Most of the doors have seen better days, and I can feel the heat of the fire through the hallway. It's not quite like being in an oven, but it's certainly an unpleasant sauna. The doors don't all fall apart, but none of them fit neatly into the frame, and they're all thoroughly blackened.

I check each one. She has to be behind one of them. The damage isn't as bad down here. Surely, she's still alive. She has to be.

Near the last door, I find something. There's another door past it, massive and metal and red from the flames still licking at it.

I should've brought water as well as the blood. "Kalila!" I shout. "I'm here."

No sound comes from the other side.

This is going to hurt. I set the blood down and step through waist-high flames, having to step over some brittle bones that must've been Reynolds's. I grab the door and yank it open with all my strength.

There's a sickening stench, and I find exactly what I hoped for. She's there. Not exactly alive but solid enough that I can fix her. She never could stay in one piece. Her arm came with the door.

I haul her out, knowing it must be agony, but if I can get her to the hallway, the fire isn't as bad there.

As I set her down, she doesn't make a noise. I pinch open her mouth, open the tub of blood, and pour it down her throat. It's scalding hot, and drinking it must be agonizing, though I suppose I'll find that out myself soon. My hands are more blister than flesh after dealing with that door, and I suspect the rest of me isn't much better, but I can hardly feel it. I'm not sure if that's out of concern for her or simply the third-degree burns.

I have to go through a whole quarter of the tub before there's so much as a fleshy hint to her cheeks, but her chest rises. I keep pouring, and she coughs, blood spraying on my chest.

At that cue, I take a gulp of it myself. It burns exactly as I'd feared, but it tastes amazing. I can't imagine where he got this. It's like no blood I've ever tried. It's a shame I'll never be able to find out.

She blinks but still doesn't say a word, so I pour more blood down her throat. She coughs again. It'll just have to do.

I pick her up and run out of the house, having to leap up the broken stairway, jumping right over a fire and nearly falling into another one, but we make it and collapse on the ground outside.

A few firefighters stare at us, but I tell them to ignore us and focus on the fire, and they do precisely that.

I clutch her to me, and her eyes slowly open. "Dorenia?" she asks.

God, I expected her to say her wife's name. I'm not sure how I would've handled it. "I'm here."

The crazy bitch kisses me. She just leans in, catches my lips with hers, and kisses me. Then promptly passes out.

I'm left blinking and confused, staring at her and realizing that she's naked.

I should've gotten more clothes from the cop.

Why did she kiss me? *Oh, don't give yourself that, Dorenia. You've already had this discussion with her. You know what you both want. You're much too old to start looking for signs when you already have a solid answer.* She got her revenge. It doesn't mean she's ready to move past it, but when she's delirious and half-dead, maybe that was enough for her to start.

The keys to her truck were lost in the fire along with her clothes, but I'm in good enough condition to carry her back to my place. Not for any scandalous reasons. I have blood in my fridge, and I suspect her motel lacks that amenity.

By the time we reach my condo, it feels like it should be late in the evening, but the sun is high in the sky, and it can't be much past noon. I set her on the couch, heat up some blood, and wait.

I'm not sure if it's minutes or hours. I haven't been able to take my eyes off her long enough to check. But she finally opens hers and looks around. "Where am I?"

"You're at my home," I say. "Drink your blood. You need it."

She stares at me for a long moment, then looks at the cup on the table beside her and drains it in a single gulp. "Fuck. You're okay?"

"How are you worried about me after you were baked in a steel box?"

"You ran through fire. There was barely anything left of you."

I sigh, smiling. I've been sitting in the armchair beside the couch rather than on it with her. Maybe I don't feel right being so close to her when she probably doesn't even know she kissed me. I didn't think about it when I came in. I just sat down. "You're one to talk. How many times have I had to save your life now?"

She smiles, staring at the empty, bloodstained cup. "A girl could get used to it, you know?"

"Oh, you think I'm always going to be there to save your ass when you do something this stupid?"

She meets my eyes, and I try not to gaze into hers like a lovesick schoolgirl. "You sure seem to be so far. Does it seem likely you'll stop?"

"I'm not following you from town to town while you hunt vampires. I have a business to run."

She licks her lips, sits up, and sets the cup down, but she doesn't move past that. She simply stays there, not quite looking at me. "Well, there are a lot of monsters here."

"There are. Though we tend to call them fiends."

"Not the ones I hunt. I think they earn the title."

"I suppose you have a point. Though I thought you were worried you haven't always hunted bad monsters."

She sighs and shrugs. "Maybe. But I know there are still plenty that are a threat to people, and I know that I can do something about them. I suppose Toronto is as good a place as any to do it, maybe better, given how they congregate here."

"So, what, you want to move in with me?"

Her eyes widen, and if she'd still been drinking, she'd have done a spit take. "I wasn't! No. I…I thought maybe I could stay in Toronto for a while, and we could maybe, if you want, see where this goes."

"Well, I suppose we did already kiss."

I didn't realize her eyes could get wider. "We…What? When? No."

I chuckle. "You kissed me the first time you came to."

She gulps and stares at herself, seeming to finally realize that she's naked. She wraps an arm over her chest. "I…Damn, you couldn't have gotten me a blanket or something?"

"Trying to change the subject."

"I mean, if you wanted to enjoy the view…"

I shake my head. "I wasn't thinking about it. I'd been sick with worry over you. I'm sorry. I should've. I wasn't trying to catch a peek."

"It's fine," she mutters. "I probably could've averted my eyes better when you were in the same position earlier. I…Um. Can I borrow some clothes?"

Chuckling, I point toward my bedroom. "Yeah. I'm sorry I wasn't able to save your jacket."

"It's okay." She disappears from the couch, and I hear her rummaging through my drawers. She's so awkward. It's adorable. I'm honestly not sure she actually knows how to date. Where would I take her? What would I even do?

Well, I suppose I have quite a while to find out.

She comes out wearing a white dress shirt that looks so much better on her than it ever did on me, and a pair of exercise pants that seem a bit tight for her. "Thanks," she mutters, staring studiously at my carpet.

I stand and with only a moment's hesitation, walk over to her. "It's okay."

"What is?" She looks up, meeting my eyes.

"I guess everything. But I meant that there's nothing to be worried about. We got our revenge. We're safe. And we both clearly have a thing for each other. So let's try to relax. Besides, we should celebrate. We made Toronto a lot safer, and now maybe your wife can finally rest."

She nods, but I see a twinge of guilt. "Yeah."

"Let's order takeout and have a night in. I promise, there will always be more vampires to kill, but for now, you need to rest."

"No, you're right. I do. Though, fuck, what day is it?"

"Friday. Why?"

"Damn, thought that might actually get me out of an awkward moment." She grins. "All right, well, I have an obligation tomorrow, but I suppose I'm all yours tonight."

I stare at her. "An obligation? Who on earth invited you to anything? You tend to kill everyone."

"Unfortunately, I owe a demon a poker game."

"You what?"

She chuckles. "Yeah, believe me, I'd prefer the killing." She sits on my couch and pats the seat next to her. "I'll tell you all about it. It might've actually saved our asses earlier, as it was part of what got Cleaver—Chuck—out of attacking us. Well, I guess saved *his* ass more than ours."

"Well, you know I love a good story."

She smirks. "And I know you love food."

"I can take a hint." I chuckle and grab my phone. "Indian sound good?"

"Sure."

I call the place and find out that our food should be here in forty-five minutes, then I sit and have a normal conversation with the crazy vampire hunter I've been crushing on. We talk about our lives, our families, and occasionally, even that poker game the story was supposed to be about, but by the time we're finally done, we've demolished two entire meals, and the sun is well past set.

I shouldn't kiss her. I know I shouldn't. She's not ready for it.

She squeezes my hand. "Just give me some time," she says.

I nod.

She doesn't kiss me. At least not properly. But her lips press against my cheek, and my heart absolutely melts. God, I really am falling for this girl.

EPILOGUE

Dorenia

I let out a deep breath, staring at the building, trying not to let my fear show.

Apparently, I fail because Kalila takes my arm. "What are you worried about? You see them all the time."

"Yeah, but you don't."

Her fangs show in a wicked smile. She's enjoying my pain. "That's very sweet. Are you sure you want me here for this? You're already showing them their new home. That's quite a lot. They don't need to meet me now too."

"I'm going to introduce them to my girlfriend." I glare at her. "Or are you trying to get out of it?"

She holds her hands up in surrender, but her smile only grows. The last few months dating her have been absolutely magical. I wasn't a hundred-percent convinced she was ready, but she's been managing remarkably well. Maybe I'd been the one looking for an excuse. Now, meeting my family, it makes it feel all the more official.

I pull away from her arm and grip her hand. It'll be okay. We'll be fine. I groan. "They wouldn't even let me pick them up at the airport."

"Aren't there, like, dozens of them? That hardly seems practical."

"Well, yeah, but I could've chartered a bus or something. It would've been fine."

"You already bought an entire apartment complex for them. I'm sure they want to contribute as well, even if it only means paying for their own plane tickets and bus fare."

I glower at her.

She kisses my cheek, and my anxiety vanishes. She's so lucky she has that effect on me.

We wait. And we wait.

"Should we check the bus stop?" I ask.

She squeezes my hand. "I think they can manage to take a bus on their own."

"Yeah, but—"

"Dorenia, it'll be fine. It's safe now. You don't have some stupid asshole wanting to kill them for knowing you, and you found a fantastic neighborhood and completely spoil them. And maybe they'll even tolerate me. Please, relax. I've got you."

I nod, doing my best to believe her. It's hard. I've kept them away from here for so long because of what that monster might do. And now I'm expecting them to meet a different vampire and to simply be fine with it. Sure, they all know, and none of them have any issue with me. But it's hard to go, "Hey, extended family, this is my girlfriend, the murderous vampire. Don't worry, she's a good murderer. She killed that asshole who was terrorizing us for your entire lives."

Actually, that doesn't sound as bad as I thought it would. I should probably lead with the last part, though.

She squeezes my hand again, and my heart stops. Or maybe it already had. Sometimes it bothers to beat, but it's always so unpredictable.

"Are you sure the apartments are nice enough?" I ask. "I only got them some basic furniture because I wanted them to be able to choose how they wanted things. I should've bought more and let them decide what they didn't want."

"I think they'll be happy just to be here, and this is the most extravagant gift anyone has ever given anyone."

"Well, they're uprooting themselves from their homes to come out here. I couldn't *not* give them a place to live."

Her thumb brushes over my knuckles. "They'll love it."

"Okay." I take a deep breath and sigh. "You're right."

Finally, I smell them approaching. Their footsteps echo through the streets. There are other pedestrians but not in groups of dozens all walking together. I'd know it was them even if they didn't smell like home.

They grow close enough to see. I beam at them, waving eagerly for them to hurry up and get over here. They're actually here.

And they're about to meet Kalila.

Oh my God. Why did I think this was a good idea?

This is awful. She should go.

No, I can't hide her from them. And I've already said they'll be meeting her.

I force my smile back on as they approach. "Wow, so this is it?" Airant says. I think he's technically not related to me, but I always think of the whole caravan as my family, and at this point, it's been so many generations that they may well all actually be. "I hadn't thought it'd be this big. This whole place is for us?"

I nod, grinning genuinely again. "Yeah, let me give you the grand tour." I blink. "Actually, I'm not sure we can all fit in an apartment, now that I think about it, so I'm not sure how I'd show you all." I'd wanted the apartment for its communal areas, but I hadn't considered how the individual apartments would affect their tour. There's a gorgeous center area with a firepit—which is still smoking from the brisket and veggies we just finished cooking—built-in grills, some old picnic tables that I polished and a few new ones, and a pool. While we never had a pool, the whole setup reminds me so much of what meals were like growing up that I knew it was the perfect choice. We can be a family again. "Well, the keys are on the table there." I point. "I guess you can take a look for yourselves? Oh, but you must be starving from the long trip. Did you want to eat first?"

"It smells amazing," Mala says. Not my Mala, though she was named for her. "Sure, we can figure out the rooms later."

It doesn't take much more for them to all head straight to the delicious scents of the roasting food. "Thank you for doing all this," Airant says.

"It's only what you deserve after all I've put you through."

"You've never put us through anything we didn't volunteer for." He clasps my hand. "We're family. Now, how about you introduce us to this lovely young lady as the little ones get their plates?"

"I'm young now?" Kalila asks. "Damn, and every waitress assumed you were my younger sister. Except that one who thought you were my daughter."

I roll my eyes. "You're young compared to me."

"Not him, though." She holds her hand out. "I'm Kalila Yassin."

He grins. "So I've heard. She's told me so much about you. I'm glad someone is keeping our girl satisfied."

"Airant!"

He chortles and only smiles wider as he beckons the others over to gawk at my girlfriend. By the time they're all finished meeting her, the food is nearly gone, so I hurry over to collect what's left while she chatters away with my family, and they all sort out seating.

"No, you've done enough. Go relax," Mala says.

"I wasn't even doing anything more. I was just going to make a couple plates."

Mala rolls her eyes. "Well, that's a miracle. I was sure you were going to start cleaning up or do your normal workaholic thing. Go sit. I'll make them." She gives me a quick smile. "Go save your partner from the kids."

I stare at her and look over at where the children have clustered at one table, all talking to Kalila. Ferka is wearing the new leather jacket I bought Kalila, which is the size of almost her whole body, and a few other kids are tugging at it for their own turn while Kalila animatedly describes something that I at first assume to be one of her monster hunting adventures, but once the words filter through the other conversations, I realize that she's describing the solar system and listing all the planets, dwarf planets, and orbiting bodies.

God, I forgot I was dating an astrophysicist. I should take her stargazing sometime.

I approach them, and Kalila's already ecstatic expression somehow grows even happier, her eyes lighting up at the sight of me. Well, at least I'm not the only one head-over-heels in this relationship. She scooches over, and I wrap an arm around her, sitting and listening to her go on about the solar system and eventually about other stars once we've been given our food.

It's perfect. The food too, not to toot my own horn, but I never thought I'd have this again. I have my family back, and I think she's starting to feel that she might, too. I know it'll never be the same as what she lost, and I'm not going to bring it up if she's not the one to start it, but I can see how much this means to her.

Who would've thought the half-dead, blood-crazed vampire who saved my life a few months ago would be such a family woman? I kiss her cheek, and she stops mid-sentence to look confused at me before I give her a more proper, though chaste, kiss and remind her to eat some of her food.

She does, but it hardly stops her from talking to the kids. She's a terrible influence on them, though I suspect they'd be talking with their mouths full either way.

Eventually, I get dragged away by Airant and a few others for drinks, but Kalila says she'll look after the kids. I'm not sure if she's just too excited to get a sample of reliving both her teaching and mothering or if she's trying to get out of drinking. Probably mostly the former.

We sip beers and watch the sunset while Fowk pushes his new homemade mead on me, but I'm not foolish enough to try that again. I was throwing up blood until the next morning last time.

"She seems nice," he says after my third refusal.

It's so weird to think of her that way, but I don't want to insist that my partner isn't nice, so I nod. "Yeah. I guess she is."

"And you're happy with her?" Airant asks.

"I am."

He wraps his arm around my shoulders and shakes me happily. "I don't think I've ever seen you happy before."

"I have been," I insist.

He shrugs. "I guess I don't see you that often, then."

"Well, I'm always happy when I visit you all."

"Other than looking guilty as all hell," Fowk says. "You know it's not your fault that he was after us."

"It was."

"I know the story."

I sigh and shrug away, watching Kalila with the kids while I finish my beer. "She took care of him. He's never going to bother us again."

"And you never found out who he was?"

I shake my head. "I suppose it didn't matter. He was a monster. It doesn't make me one, just like it doesn't matter how old Reynolds actually was." I grind my teeth. I hate how many loose ends we're left with. My entire stock-in-trade is knowing things, and all these months later, I've still barely managed to piece together anything. It doesn't help that most of his records burnt down with his house. Going over the books and history, I found that he seemed to have been in Toronto back when I got here, but he went to the US at some point, and that's where things get fuzzy.

"That doesn't sound much like you."

I groan and grab another beer. "I'm trying to convince myself. I'm glad they're gone, though. I did tell you about Reynolds, right?"

"Her equivalent of our bogeyman, yeah," Airant says.

"Don't call him that," I mutter.

"Why? It seems pretty dead-on."

I glare at him, but he remains undeterred. Great, I suppose I can't exactly point out that I'm not a monster and then expect my family to be scared of me.

As the evening grows into night, most of the humans end up going to bed, and I can hear them marveling at their new homes. I try not to let it go to my head. I'm left with only Kalila and a few scattered people drinking and talking quietly. I lie on the picnic table, looking up at the stars. The light pollution makes them hard to see, but a few still stand out. I tug her hand and get her to lie with me.

I turn from the stars and look into her eyes. They still have that same effect on me. "I think it went well."

"It went amazingly. I love your family," she says.

God, if we'd been dating for longer, I'd make some smooth remark about her joining it, but I suppose there's always time. I kiss her and cup her cheek, running my thumb along her jaw. "I'm so glad you came here."

"I think it worked out pretty well for everyone. Well, except the ones I killed." She grins and kisses my thumb.

I giggle. "I'd say they're better off too."

"Maybe."

I turn back to the sky and pull her closer, resting her head on my chest, and point up at the stars. "What's that constellation?"

"I don't really know constellations. I would use a chart for that."

"Seriously? What's your use, then?" I run my fingers through her hair.

She playfully pulls away but stays put when I offer the slightest resistance. "I suppose I could at least point out a few I know, and it looks like Venus is visible."

"I guess that'll suffice," I whine, trying to sound as pouty as I can manage in her arms.

She points out Polaris and uses it to show the two dippers and Orion and then helps me find Venus and goes off on a tangent about it while I hold her, trying to take it all in.

We probably should go home and sleep. I told her I'd join her in clearing out some gorgons tomorrow, and I'm still not sure if they can affect us. I bought some mirrored sunglasses just in case, and I'm hoping that'll be enough. Either way, I'm sure I'll be all right. I have her to watch my back. I just have to keep her alive to do so. God, I really did luck out.

About the Author

Genevieve McCluer was born in California and grew up in numerous cities across the country. She studied criminal justice in college but, after a few years of that, moved her focus to writing. Her whole life, she's been obsessed with mythology, and she bases her stories in those myths.

She now lives in Arizona with her partner and cats, working away at far too many novels. In her free time she pesters the cats, plays video games, and attempts to be better at archery.

GenevieveMcCluer.com
GenevieveMcCluer@gmail.com

Books Available from Bold Strokes Books

Cold Blood by Genevieve McCluer. Maybe together, Kalila and Dorenia have a chance of taking down the vampires who have eluded them all these years. And maybe, in each other, they can find a love worth living for. (978-1-63679-195-1)

Greener Pastures by Aurora Rey. When city girl and CPA Audrey Adams finds herself tending her aunt's farm, will Rowan Marshall—the charming cider maker next door—turn out to be her saving grace or the bane of her existence? (978-1-63679-116-6)

Grounded by Amanda Radley. For a second chance, Olivia and Emily will need to accept their mistakes, learn to communicate properly, and with a little help from five-year-old Henry, fall madly in love all over again. Sequel to Flight SQA016. (978-1-63679-241-5)

Journey's End by Amanda Radley. In this heartwarming conclusion to the Flight series, Olivia and Emily must finally decide what they want, what they need, and how to follow the dreams of their hearts. (978-1-63679-233-0)

Pursued: Lillian's Story by Felice Picano. Fleeing a disastrous marriage to the Lord Exchequer of England, Lillian of Ravenglass reveals an incident-filled, often bizarre, tale of great wealth and power, perfidy, and betrayal. (978-1-63679-197-5)

Secret Agent by Michelle Larkin. CIA agent Peyton North embarks on a global chase to apprehend rogue agent Zoey Blackwood, but her commitment to the mission is tested as the sparks between them ignite and their sizzling attraction approaches a point of no return. (978-1-63555-753-4)

Something Between Us by Krystina Rivers. A decade after her heart was broken under Don't Ask, Don't Tell, Kirby runs into her first love and has to decide if what's still between them is enough to heal her broken heart. (978-1-63679-135-7)

Sugar Girl by Emma L McGeown. Having traded in traditional romance for the perks of Sugar Dating, Ciara Reilly not only enjoys the no-strings-attached arrangement, she's also a hit with her clients. That is until she meets the beautiful entrepreneur Charlie Keller who makes her want to go sugar-free. (978-1-63679-156-2)

The Business of Pleasure by Ronica Black. Editor in chief Valerie Raffield is quickly becoming smitten by Lennox, the graphic artist she's hired to work remotely. But when Lennox doesn't show for their first face-to-face meeting, Valerie's heart and her business may be in jeopardy. (978-1-63679-134-0)

The Hummingbird Sanctuary by Erin Zak. The Hummingbird Sanctuary, Colorado's hottest resort destination: Come for the mountains, stay for the charm, and enjoy the drama as Olive, Eleanor, and Harriet figure out the meaning of true friendship. (978-1-63679-163-0)

The Witch Queen's Mate by Jennifer Karter. Barra and Silvi must overcome their ingrained hatred and prejudice to use Barra's magic and save both their peoples, not just from slavery, but destruction. (978-1-63679-202-6)

With a Twist by Georgia Beers. Starting over isn't easy for Amelia Martini. When the irritatingly cheerful Kirby Dupress comes into her life will Amelia be brave enough to go after the love she really wants? (978-1-63555-987-3)

Business of the Heart by Claire Forsythe. When a hopeless romantic meets a tough-as-nails cynic, they'll need to overcome the wounds of the past to discover that their hearts are the most important business of all. (978-1-63679-167-8)

Dying for You by Jenny Frame. Can Victorija Dred keep an age-old vow and fight the need to take blood from Daisy Macdougall? (978-1-63679-073-2)

Exclusive by Melissa Brayden. Skylar Ruiz lands the TV reporting job of a lifetime, but is she willing to sacrifice it all for the love of her longtime crush, anchorwoman Carolyn McNamara? (978-1-63679-112-8)

Her Duchess to Desire by Jane Walsh. An up-and-coming interior designer seeks to create a happily ever after with an intriguing duchess, proving that love never goes out of fashion. (978-1-63679-065-7)

Murder on Monte Vista by David S. Pederson. Private Detective Mason Adler's angst at turning fifty is forgotten when his "birthday present," the handsome, young Henry Bowtrickle, turns up dead, and it's up to Mason to figure out who did it, and why. (978-1-63679-124-1)

Take Her Down by Lauren Emily Whalen. Stakes are cutthroat, scheming is creative, and loyalty is ever-changing in this queer, female-driven YA retelling of Shakespeare's Julius Caesar. (978-1-63679-089-3)

The Game by Jan Gayle. Ryan Gibbs is a talented golfer, but her guilt means she may never leave her small town, even if Katherine Reese tempts her with competition and passion. (978-1-63679-126-5)

Whereabouts Unknown by Meredith Doench. While homicide detective Theodora Madsen recovers from a potentially career-ending injury, she scrambles to solve the cases of two missing sixteen-year-old girls from Ohio. (978-1-63555-647-6)

Boy at the Window by Lauren Melissa Ellzey. Daniel Kim struggles to hold onto reality while haunted by both his very-present past and his never-present parents. Jiwon Yoon may be the only one who can break Daniel free. (978-1-63679-092-3)

Deadly Secrets by VK Powell. Corporate criminals want whistleblower Jana Elliott permanently silenced, but Rafe Silva will risk everything to keep the woman she loves safe. (978-1-63679-087-9)

Enchanted Autumn by Ursula Klein. When Elizabeth comes to Salem, Massachusetts, to study the witch trials, she never expects to find love—or an actual witch…and Hazel might just turn out to be both. (978-1-63679-104-3)

Escorted by Renee Roman. When fantasy meets reality, will escort Ryan Lewis be able to walk away from a chance at forever with her new client Dani? (978-1-63679-039-8)

Her Heart's Desire by Anne Shade. Two women. One choice. Will Eve and Lynette be able to overcome their doubts and fears to embrace their deepest desire? (978-1-63679-102-9)

My Secret Valentine by Julie Cannon, Erin Dutton, & Anne Shade. Winning the heart of your secret Valentine? These award-winning authors agree, there is no better way to fall in love. (978-1-63679-071-8)

Perilous Obsession by Carsen Taite. When reporter Macy Moran becomes consumed with solving a cold case, will her quest for the truth bring her closer to Detective Beck Ramsey or will her obsession with finding a murderer rob her of a chance at true love? (978-1-63679-009-1)

Reading Her by Amanda Radley. Lauren and Allegra learn love and happiness are right where they least expect it. There's just one problem: Lauren has a secret she cannot tell anyone, and Allegra knows she's hiding something. (978-1-63679-075-6)

The Willing by Lyn Hemphill. Kitty Wilson doesn't know how, but she can bring people back from the dead as long as someone is willing to take their place and keep the universe in balance. (978-1-63679-083-1)

Three Left Turns to Nowhere by Nathan Burgoine, J. Marshall Freeman, & Jeffrey Ricker. Three strangers heading to a convention in Toronto are stranded in rural Ontario, where a small town with a subtle kind of magic leads each to discover what he's been searching for. (978-1-63679-050-3)

Watching Over Her by Ronica Black. As they face the snowstorm of the century, and the looming threat of a stalker, Riley and Zoey just might find love in the most unexpected of places. (978-1-63679-100-5)

#shedeservedit by Greg Herren. When his gay best friend, and high school football star, is murdered, Alex Wheeler is a suspect and must find the truth to clear himself. (978-1-63555-996-5)

Always by Kris Bryant. When a pushy American private investigator shows up demanding to meet the woman in Camila's artwork, instead of introducing her to her great-grandmother, Camila decides to lead her on a wild goose chase all over Italy. (978-1-63679-027-5)

Exes and O's by Joy Argento. Ali and Madison really only have one thing in common. The girl who broke their heart may be the only one who can put it back together. (978-1-63679-017-6)

One Verse Multi by Sander Santiago. Life was good: promotion, friends, falling in love, discovering that the multi-verse is on a fast track to collision—wait, what? Good thing Martin King works for a company that can fix the problem, right...um...right? (978-1-63679-069-5)

Paris Rules by Jaime Maddox. Carly Becker has been searching for the perfect woman all her life, but no one ever seems to be just right until Paige Waterford checks all her boxes, except the most important one—she's married. (978-1-63679-077-0)

Shadow Dancers by Suzie Clarke. In this third and final book in the Moon Shadow series, Rachel must find a way to become the hunter and not the hunted, and this time she will meet Ehsee Yumiko head-on. (978-1-63555-829-6)

The Kiss by C.A. Popovich. When her wife refuses their divorce and begins to stalk her, threatening her life, Kate realizes to protect her new love, Leslie, she has to let her go, even if it breaks her heart. (978-1-63679-079-4)

The Wedding Setup by Charlotte Greene. When Ryann, a big-time New York executive, goes to Colorado to help out with her best friend's wedding, she never expects to fall for the maid of honor. (978-1-63679-033-6)

Velocity by Gun Brooke. Holly and Claire work toward an uncertain future preparing for an alien space mission, and only one thing is for certain, they will have to risk their lives, and their hearts, to discover the truth. (978-1-63555-983-5)

Wildflower Words by Sam Ledel. Lida Jones treks West with her father in search of a better life on the rapidly developing American frontier, but finds home when she meets Hazel Thompson. (978-1-63679-055-8)

A Fairer Tomorrow by Kathleen Knowles. For Maddie Weeks and Gerry Stern, the Second World War brought them together, but the end of the war might rip them apart. (978-1-63555-874-6)

Holiday Hearts by Diana Day-Admire and Lyn Cole. Opposites attract during Christmastime chaos in Kansas City. (978-1-63679-128-9)

Changing Majors by Ana Hartnett Reichardt. Beyond a love, beyond a coming-out, Bailey Sullivan discovers what lies beyond the shame and self-doubt imposed on her by traditional Southern ideals. (978-1-63679-081-7)

Fresh Grave in Grand Canyon by Lee Patton. The age-old Grand Canyon becomes more and more ominous as a group of volunteers fight to survive alone in nature and uncover a murderer among them. (978-1-63679-047-3)

Highland Whirl by Anna Larner. Opposites attract in the Scottish Highlands, when feisty Alice Campbell falls for city-girl-about-town Roxanne Barns. (978-1-63555-892-0)

Humbug by Amanda Radley. With the corporate Christmas party in jeopardy, CEO Rosalind Caldwell hires Christmas Girl Ellie Pearce as her personal assistant. The only problem is, Ellie isn't a PA, has never planned a party, and develops a ridiculous crush on her totally intimidating new boss. (978-1-63555-965-1)

On the Rocks by Georgia Beers. Schoolteacher Vanessa Martini makes no apologies for her dating checklist, and newly single mom Grace Chapman ticks all Vanessa's Do Not Date boxes. Of course, they're never going to fall in love. (978-1-63555-989-7)

Song of Serenity by Brey Willows. Arguing with the Muse of music and justice is complicated, falling in love with her even more so. (978-1-63679-015-2)

The Christmas Proposal by Lisa Moreau. Stranded together in a Christmas village on a snowy mountain, Grace and Bridget face their past and question their dreams for the future. (978-1-63555-648-3)

The Infinite Summer by Morgan Lee Miller. While spending the summer with her dad in a small beach town, Remi Brenner falls for Harper Hebert and accidentally finds herself tangled up in an intense restaurant rivalry between her famous stepmom and her first love. (978-1-63555-969-9)

Wisdom by Jesse J. Thoma. When Sophia and Reggie are chosen for the governor's new community design team and tasked with tackling substance abuse and mental health issues, battle lines are drawn even as sparks fly. (978-1-63555-886-9)